You are Lone Wolf — last of the Kai Lords of Sommerlund, and sole survivor of the massacre that destroyed them during a bitter war with your age-old enemies, the Darklords of Helgedad.

The Zakhan of Vassagonia, the imperial ruler of this desert empire, has sent his most trusted envoy to seek a treaty of peace between your two countries, and the king has asked you to sign the treaty on behalf of your country.

You wave farewell to Holmgard on this bleak midwinter's day, feeling sure you will return before the thaw. But as you watch the spires of Holmgard disappear in the falling snow, you have no inkling of the shadow that awaits you in Vassagonia.

JOE DEVER, the author of the *Lone Wolf* series, is a contributing editor to *White Dwarf*, Britain's leading fantasy games magazine. *Lone Wolf* is the culmination of seven years of developing the world of Magnamund. He is currently at work on a huge compendium based on the world of Magnamund.

GARY CHALK, the illustrator of the *Lone Wolf* series, was working as a children's book illustrator when he became involved in adventure gaming, an interest which eventually led to the creation of several successful games. He is the inventor/illustrator of some of Britain's biggest-selling fantasy games.

Book 5

Shadow on the Sand

Including *two* Lone Wolf adventures

Joe Dever

Illustrated by Gary Chalk

Pacer BOOKS FOR YOUNG ADULTS

BERKLEY BOOKS, NEW YORK

For Robert Alfred Dever (1917–65)
and William Roland Chalk

ACTION CHART

KAI DISCIPLINES	NOTES
1	
2	
3	
4	
5	

BONUS KAI DISCIPLINES

6	
6th Discipline if you've completed 1 Lone Wolf adventure successfully	
7	
7th Discipline if you've completed 2 Lone Wolf adventures successfully	
8	
8th Discipline if you've completed 3 Lone Wolf adventures successfully	
9	
9th Discipline if you've completed 4 Lone Wolf adventures successfully	

BACKPACK (max 8 articles)	MEALS
1	
2	
3	—3 EP if no Meal available when instructed to eat.
4	BELT POUCH (50 maximum) Containing Gold Crowns
5	
6	
7	
8 Can be discarded when not in combat.	

EP = ENDURANCE POINTS   CS = COMBAT SKILL
(SEE OVER PAGE FOR SPECIAL ITEMS)

COMBAT SKILL

ENDURANCE POINTS

Can never go above initial score
0 = dead

COMBAT RECORD

LONE WOLF	COMBAT RATIO	ENEMY

LONE WOLF	COMBAT RATIO	ENEMY

LONE WOLF	COMBAT RATIO	ENEMY

LONE WOLF	COMBAT RATIO	ENEMY

LONE WOLF	COMBAT RATIO	ENEMY

LONE WOLF	COMBAT RATIO	ENEMY

KAI RANK

SPECIAL ITEMS
AND WEAPONS LIST

DESCRIPTION	KNOWN EFFECTS

WEAPONS (maximum 2 Weapons)

1	
2	

If holding Weapon and appropriate Weaponskill in combat +2 CS.
If combat entered carrying no Weapon —4 CS.

THE STORY SO FAR . . .

You are Lone Wolf – last of the Kai Lords of Sommerlund, and sole survivor of the massacre that destroyed them during a bitter war with your age-old enemies, the Darklords of Helgedad.

It is mid-winter in your northern homeland and a mantle of snow lies knee-deep in the streets of Holmgard – the capital – when you are summoned from your monastery in the hills by a messenger bearing a scroll, signed and sealed by the hand of King Ulnar. You are surprised to read the king's message, for it is a request for your help in solving an urgent problem of what he describes as 'great diplomatic importance'. It seems a strange request to make of a warrior lord, whose skills are better suited to the field of battle than to parleying with foreign envoys. However, you obey the summons and upon your arrival at the capital, all is made clear.

The Zakhan of Vassagonia, the imperial ruler of this desert empire, has sent his most trusted envoy to seek a treaty of peace between your two countries, and you have been asked to sign the treaty on behalf of your country. The reason for this is easily apparent.

Less than a year ago, a renegade noble of Vassagonia called Barraka led his army of bandits in an attack upon the Sommlending province of Ruanon. This mining town and much of the surrounding land was overrun and destroyed. Many Sommlending lost their lives, and many more were enslaved and forced to labour in the mines of the Maaken range. When the regular convoy from Ruanon failed to arrive at the capital, the king sent you to investigate. A great battle ensued in which you defeated Barraka in mortal combat. Without your courage and skill, the safety of Sommerlund and all of the Lastlands would have been placed in grave peril.

'Your majesty, the Zakhan is gravely embarrassed by Barraka's foul treachery, and is most anxious that our friendship and trust be restored. He begs that you send the Kai warrior, Lone Wolf, to sign a treaty of peace with him at the Grand Palace in Barrakeesh,' whimpers the Zakhan's emissary, as he kneels at the feet of King Ulnar.

The king rises from his throne, barely able to conceal his distaste for the fawning envoy. He turns his gaze to you and bids you follow him to the privacy of an antechamber.

'I have no liking for this desert realm, Lone Wolf, but I like the prospect of war even less. The Zakhan is old and frail, and has no son to claim his throne when he dies. Barraka was but one of many ruthless nobles who wait like jackals for the chance to seize power, and I fear they grow too impatient to allow the Zakhan to die a natural death. The treaty may not guarantee peace with Vassagonia once the Zakhan is dead, but it will at least buy us precious time to strengthen our southern border.'

The king leads you to a window and points towards the harbour, barely visible through the falling snow.

10

A Vassagonian galley lies anchored close to the harbour wall.

'Go to Vassagonia, Lone Wolf. Sign the treaty and return quickly. Even with the promise of peace, I fear the shadow of war will fall upon us before the year is out.'

You wave farewell to Holmgard on this bleak mid-winter's day, feeling sure you will return before the thaw. But as you watch the spires of Holmgard disappear in the falling snow, you have no inkling of the shadow that awaits you in Vassagonia.

THE GAME RULES

You keep a record of your adventure on the *Action Chart* that you will find in the front of this book. For further adventuring you can copy out the chart yourself or get it photocopied.

During your training as a Kai Lord you have developed fighting prowess – COMBAT SKILL and physical stamina – ENDURANCE. Before you set off on your adventure you need to measure how effective your training has been. To do this take a pencil and, with your eyes closed, point with the blunt end of it on to the *Random Number Table* on the last page of this book. If you pick *0* it counts as zero.

The first number that you pick from the *Random Number Table* in this way represents your COMBAT SKILL. Add 10 to the number you picked and write the total in the COMBAT SKILL section of your *Action Chart*. (ie, if your pencil fell on the number 4 in the *Random Number Table* you would write in a COMBAT SKILL of 14.) When you fight, your COMBAT SKILL will be pitted against that of your enemy. A high score in this section is therefore very desirable.

The second number that you pick from the *Random Number Table* represents your powers of ENDURANCE. Add 20 to this number and write the total in the ENDURANCE section of your *Action Chart*. (ie, if your pencil fell on the number 6 on the *Random Number Table* you would have 26 ENDURANCE points.)

If you are wounded in combat you will lose ENDURANCE points. If at any time your ENDURANCE points fall to zero, you are dead and the adventure is over. Lost ENDURANCE points can be regained during the course of the adventure, but your number of ENDURANCE points can never rise above the number you started with.

If you have successfully completed any of the previous adventures in the Lone Wolf series, you will already have your Combat Skill, Endurance Points and Kai Disciplines which you can now carry over with you to Book 5. You may also carry over any Weapons and Special Items that you held at the end of your last adventure, and these should be entered on your new Action Chart (you are still limited to two Weapons and eight Backpack Items).

You may choose one bonus Kai Discipline to add to your Action Chart for every Lone Wolf adventure you have successfully completed; now read the section on equipment for Book 5 carefully.

KAI DISCIPLINES

Over the centuries, the Kai monks have mastered the skills of the warrior. These skills are known as the Kai Disciplines, and they are taught to all Kai Lords. You are a Kai initiate which means that you have learnt only *five* of the skills listed below. The choice of which five skills these are, is for you to make. As all of the disciplines will be of use to you at some point on your adventure, pick your five with care. The correct use of a discipline at the right time can save your life.

When you have chosen your five disciplines, enter them in the Kai Discipline section of your *Action Chart*.

Camouflage

This discipline enables a Kai Lord to blend in with his surroundings. In the countryside, he can hide undetected among trees and rocks and pass close to an enemy without being seen. In a town or city, it helps him to look and sound like a native of that area, and can help him to find shelter or a safe hiding place.

If you choose this skill, write 'Camouflage' on your *Action Chart*.

Hunting

This skill ensures that a Kai Lord will never starve in the wild. He will always be able to hunt for food for himself except in areas of wasteland and desert. You are aware that most of Vassagonia is arid desert; should your adventure lead you into this desert, the opportunities for successful hunting may not arise. But this skill is still very useful for it enables a Kai Lord to move with great speed and dexterity.

If you choose this skill, write 'Hunting' on your *Action Chart*.

14

Sixth Sense

This skill may warn a Kai Lord of imminent danger. It may also reveal the true purpose of a stranger or strange object encountered in your adventure.

If you choose this skill, write 'Sixth Sense' on your *Action Chart*.

Tracking

This skill enables a Kai Lord to make the correct choice of a path in the wild, to discover the location of a person or object in a town or city and to read the secrets of footprints or tracks.

If you choose this skill, write 'Tracking' on your *Action Chart*.

Healing

This discipline can be used to restore ENDURANCE points lost in combat. If you possess this skill, you may restore 1 ENDURANCE point to your total for every numbered section of the book you pass through in which you are not involved in combat. (This is only to be used after your ENDURANCE has fallen below its original level.) Remember that your ENDURANCE cannot rise above its original level.

If you choose this skill, write 'Healing: + 1 ENDURANCE point for each section without combat' on your *Action Chart*.

Weaponskill

Upon entering the Kai monastery, each initiate was taught to master one type of weapon. If Weaponskill is to be one of your Kai Disciplines, pick a number in

15

the usual way from the *Random Number Table* on the last page of the book, and then find the corresponding weapon from the list below. This is the weapon in which you have skill. When you enter combat carrying this weapon, you add 2 points to your COMBAT SKILL.

0 = DAGGER

1 = SPEAR

2 = MACE

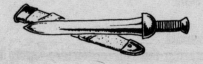

3 = SHORT SWORD

4 = WARHAMMER

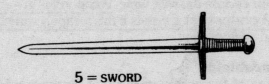

5 = SWORD

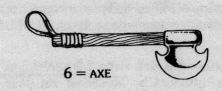

6 = AXE

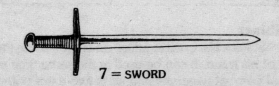

7 = SWORD

8 = QUARTERSTAFF

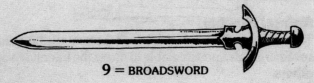

9 = BROADSWORD

The fact that you are skilled with a weapon does not mean that you set out on this adventure carrying it, but you will have opportunities to acquire weapons in the course of your adventure. You cannot carry more than 2 weapons.

If you choose this skill, write 'Weaponskill in ———— + 2 COMBAT SKILL points if this weapon carried' on your *Action Chart*.

Mindshield

Some of the hostile creatures of Magnamund have the ability to attack you using their Mindforce. The Kai Discipline of Mindshield prevents you from losing any ENDURANCE points when subjected to this form of attack.

If you choose this skill, write 'Mindshield: no points lost when attacked by Mindblast' on your *Action Chart*.

Mindblast

This enables a Kai Lord to attack an enemy using the force of his mind. It can be used at the same time as normal combat weapons and adds two extra points to your COMBAT SKILL. Not all the creatures encountered on this adventure will be harmed by Mindblast. You will be told if a creature is immune.

If you choose this skill, write 'Mindblast: + 2 COMBAT SKILL points' on your *Action Chart*.

Animal Kinship

This skill enables a Kai Lord to communicate with some animals and to be able to guess the intentions of others.

18

If you choose this skill, write 'Animal Kinship' on your *Action Chart*.

Mind Over Matter
Mastery of this discipline enables a Kai Lord to move small objects with his powers of concentration.

If you choose this skill, write 'Mind Over Matter' on your *Action Chart*.

If you have successfully completed Books 1–4 of the Lone Wolf series, completion of Book 5 will raise you to the rank of Kai Master. This means that you will have acquired all ten basic Kai skills.

All of the Special Items that you have found and kept during your adventures, may then be used in the Lone Wolf 'Magnakai' series, which begins with Book 6 entitled *The Kingdoms of Terror*.

EQUIPMENT

Before leaving Holmgard on your voyage to the Vassagonian capital of Barrakeesh, you are given a map of the desert empire (see the front of this book) and a pouch of gold. To find out how much gold is in the pouch, pick a number from the *Random Number Table*. Now add 10 to the number you have picked. The total equals the number of Gold Crowns inside the pouch, and you may now enter this number in the Gold Crowns section of your *Action Chart*. (If you have successfully completed previous Lone Wolf adventures, you may add this sum to the total of any Crowns you may already possess. Remember you can only carry a maximum of fifty Crowns.)

You may take your pick of the following items (in addition to those you already possess, but remember you may only carry two weapons). You may take up to four of the following:

DAGGER (Weapons)

POTION OF LAUMSPUR (Backpack Items). This potion restores 4 ENDURANCE points to your total when swallowed after combat. There is enough for one dose.

SWORD (Weapons)

SPEAR (Weapons)

2 SPECIAL RATIONS (Meals). Each of these Special Rations counts as one Meal, and each takes up one space in your Backpack.

MACE (Weapons)

SHIELD (Special Items). This adds 2 points to your COMBAT SKILL when used in combat.

List the four items that you choose on your *Action Chart*, under the heading given in brackets, and make a note of any effect it may have on your ENDURANCE points or COMBAT SKILL.

How to carry equipment

Now that you have your equipment, the following list shows you how it is carried. You don't need to make notes but you can refer back to this list in the course of your adventure.

DAGGER – carried in the hand.
POTION OF LAUMSPUR – carried in the Backpack.
SWORD – carried in the hand.
SPEAR – carried in the hand.
SPECIAL RATIONS – carried in the Backpack.
MACE – carried in the hand.
SHIELD – slung over shoulder when not in combat, otherwise carried in the hand.

How much can you carry?

Weapons
The maximum number of weapons that you may carry is *two*.

Backpack Items
These must be stored in your Backpack. Because space is limited, you may only keep a maximum of eight articles, including Meals, in your Backpack at any one time.

Special Items
Special Items are not carried in the Backpack. When you discover a Special Item, you will be told how to carry it.

Gold Crowns
These are always carried in the Belt Pouch. It will hold a maximum of fifty Crowns.

Food
Food is carried in your Backpack. Each Meal counts as one item.

Any item that may be of use and can be picked up on your adventure and entered on your *Action Chart* is given capital letters in the text. Unless you are told it is a Special Item, carry it in your Backpack.

How to use your equipment

Weapons
Weapons aid you in combat. If you have the Kai Discipline of Weaponskill and the correct weapon, it adds 2 points to your COMBAT SKILL. If you enter a combat with no weapons, deduct 4 points from your COMBAT SKILL and fight with your bare hands. If you find a weapon during the adventure, you may pick it up and use it. (Remember you can only carry two weapons at once.)

Backpack Items
During your travels you will discover various useful items which you may wish to keep. (Remember you can only carry a maximum of eight items in your Backpack at any time.) You may exchange or discard them at any point when you are not involved in combat.

Special Items

Special Items are not carried in the Backpack. When you discover a Special Item, you will be told how to carry it. If you have successfully completed previous Lone Wolf books, you may already possess Special Items. Before you begin *Shadow on the Sand*, you can choose to leave any or all of these items in 'Safe Keeping' at your Kai monastery in Sommerlund. Special Items in 'Safe Keeping' cannot be used, but also they cannot be lost during your adventure.

Gold Crowns

The currency of Sommerlund and Vassagonia is the Crown, which is a small gold coin. Whenever you kill an enemy and search the body, you may take any Gold Crowns that you find and put them in your Belt Pouch.

Food

You will need to eat regularly during your adventure. If you do not have any food when you are instructed to eat a Meal, you will lose 3 ENDURANCE points. If you have chosen the Kai Discipline of Hunting as one of your skills, you will not need to tick off a Meal when instructed to eat (unless you are in an area of desert where the opportunity for hunting is limited).

Potion of Laumspur

This is a healing potion that can restore 4 ENDURANCE points to your total when swallowed after combat. There is enough for one dose only. If you discover any other potion during the adventure, you will be informed of its effect. All potions are Backpack Items.

RULES FOR COMBAT

There will be occasions during your adventure when you have to fight an enemy. The enemy's COMBAT SKILL and ENDURANCE points are given in the text. Lone Wolf's aim in the combat is to kill the enemy by reducing his ENDURANCE points to zero while losing as few ENDURANCE points as possible himself.

At the start of a combat, enter Lone Wolf's and the enemy's ENDURANCE points in the appropriate boxes on the Combat Record section of your *Action Chart*.

The sequence for combat is as follows:

1. Add any extra points gained through your Kai Disciplines to your current COMBAT SKILL total.

2. Subtract the COMBAT SKILL of your enemy from this total. The result is your *Combat Ratio*. Enter it on the *Action Chart*.

Example
Lone Wolf (COMBAT SKILL 15) is ambushed by a Winged Devil (COMBAT SKILL 20). He is not given the opportunity to evade combat, but must stand and fight as the creature swoops down on him. Lone Wolf has the Kai Discipline of Mindblast to which the Winged Devil is not immune, so he adds 2 points to his COMBAT SKILL giving a total COMBAT SKILL of 17.

He subtracts the Winged Devil's COMBAT SKILL from his own, giving a *Combat Ratio* of −3. (17 − 20 = −3). −3 is noted on the *Action Chart* as the *Combat Ratio*.

3. When you have your *Combat Ratio*, pick a number from the *Random Number Table*.

4. Turn to the *Combat Results Table* on the inside back cover of the book. Along the top of the chart are shown the *Combat Ratio* numbers. Find the number that is the same as your *Combat Ratio* and cross-reference it with the random number that you have picked (the random numbers appear on the side of the chart). You now have the number of ENDURANCE points lost by both Lone Wolf and his enemy in this round of combat. (*E* represents points lost by the enemy; *LW* represents points lost by Lone Wolf.)

Example

The *Combat Ratio* between Lone Wolf and the Winged Devil has been established as −3. If the number taken from the *Random Number Table* is a 6, then the result of the first round of combat is:

Lone Wolf loses 3 ENDURANCE points
Winged Devil loses 6 ENDURANCE points

5. On the *Action Chart*, mark the changes in ENDURANCE points to the participants in the combat.

6. Unless otherwise instructed, or unless you have an option to evade, the next round of combat now starts.

7. Repeat the sequence from Stage 3.

This process of combat continues until the ENDURANCE points of either the enemy or Lone Wolf are reduced to zero, at which point the one with the zero score is declared dead. If Lone Wolf is dead, the adventure is over. If the enemy is dead, Lone Wolf proceeds but with his ENDURANCE points reduced.

A summary of Combat Rules appears on the page after the *Random Number Table*.

Evasion of combat

During your adventure you may be given the chance to evade combat. If you have already engaged in a round of combat and decide to evade, calculate the combat for that round in the usual manner. All points lost by the enemy as a result of that round are ignored, and you make your escape. Only Lone Wolf may lose ENDURANCE points during that round, but then that is the risk of running away! You may only evade if the text of the particular section allows you to do so.

LEVELS OF KAI TRAINING

The following table is a guide to the rank and titles that are bestowed upon Kai Lords at each stage of their training. As you successfully complete each adventure in the LONE WOLF series, you will gain an additional Kai Discipline and gradually progress towards mastery of the ten basic Kai Disciplines.

No. of Kai Disciplines mastered by Kai Lord	Kai Rank or Title
1	Novice
2	Intuite
3	Doan
4	Acolyte
5	Initiate – *You begin the Lone Wolf Adventures with this level of Kai training*
6	Aspirant
7	Guardian
8	Warmarn *or* Journeyman
9	Savant
10	Master

Beyond the ten basic skills of the Kai Master await the secrets of the higher Kai Disciplines or 'Magnakai'. By acquiring the wisdom of the Magnakai, a Kai Lord can progress towards the ultimate achievement and become a Kai Grand Master.

KAI WISDOM

Your mission is one of peaceful diplomacy – but beware! The desert empire of Vassagonia is notorious for being a land of deceit and treachery. Be on your guard at all times. Also, make notes as you progress, as you will find they will be of great help in future adventures.

Many things you find will help you in your adventure. Some Special Items will be useful in future LONE WOLF adventures and others may be red herrings of no real use at all, so be selective in what you decide to keep.

If this is your first LONE WOLF adventure, choose your Kai Disciplines with care – a wise choice and a great deal of courage should enable anyone to complete both parts of this adventure, no matter how weak his or her initial COMBAT SKILL and ENDURANCE points. Successful completion of previous LONE WOLF adventures, although an advantage, is not essential for the completion of this book.

May the spirits of your Kai Masters guide you on your perilous adventure.

Good Luck!

PART ONE

1

For twenty-five days, the Vassagonian galley sails on a steady course for its home port of Barrakeesh, with only a brief stop at the Durenese harbour of Port Bax to break a safe but monotonous voyage.

You use your time aboard the ship to good purpose, learning the Vassagonian language from the ship's crew. They are only too eager to teach you, asking only in return tales of your adventures in the Last-lands – for many of the sailors, these are the most exciting stories they have ever heard. By the time you reach Barrakeesh, you have both mastered their language and won their respect.

It is early afternoon when the ramparts of the desert capital are first sighted upon the horizon. You push your way through the cheering crew, and join the envoy at the prow of the ship. Beaming with pride, he hands you a telescope and invites you to view the land of his birth. The sight is indeed breathtaking. You stare in fascination at the golden domes, minarets and green-tiled roofs shimmering beneath the desert sun, and marvel at the splendour of the Grand Palace, which dominates this magnificent city. Then you notice that from every golden turret of the palace flutters a long, black pennant. You ask the envoy the meaning of the black flags. Horror floods across his face as he snatches the telescope from your hands. 'By the spirit of the Majhan! he is dead . . . the Zakhan is dead!'

As the bad news spreads through the ship, you pray that the peace treaty will be signed and honoured by the Zakhan's successor. However, the envoy is less than hopeful.

The harbour of Barrakeesh is deserted save for a handful of citizens clad in black, and the only sound that greets you is the toll of a funeral bell, echoing through the harbour on this day of mourning. Then a horse-drawn carriage enters the harbour square, escorted by the cavalry of the Palace Guard. It halts, and a dour man in turquoise robes steps out to meet you.

'A thousand greetings, Lone Wolf, I am Maouk, and I welcome you to our city on behalf of my master, his most sublime magnificence, Zakhan Kimah.'

The envoy gasps upon hearing the name of the new Zakhan. He turns to speak, his eyes wild with fear. 'It is a trap, you must—'

His warning is cut short by the blade of Maouk's dagger. Suddenly, scores of black-clad warriors emerge from the shadows; they are Sharnazim, elite Vassagonian bodyguards. They close in, surrounding you on every side. You must act quickly if you are to survive this deadly trap.

> If you wish to stand and fight against these overwhelming odds, turn to **36**.
>
> If you wish to surrender to Maouk and his warriors, turn to **176**.
>
> If you wish to run back to the galley, turn to **104**.

2

Breathless from the exertion of combat, you step back as the Elix finally collapses and dies. Slowly, its glass-green eyes mist over and become opaque like hard, cold jadin. Around the creature's blood-spattered throat hangs a Gold Chain and Key. You quickly discover that the Key opens the steel door of a strongroom at the far end of the apothecary.

High upon a shelf, just inside the door, you find a small box that contains what you seek – the Oede herb. Within seconds of pressing the beautiful golden leaves to your wounded shoulder, a tingling sensation engulfs your whole arm. The numbness soon fades; and both your arm and shoulder are free of the horrific Limbdeath microbes.

Sufficient Oede herb remains in the box for one further application. It is a powerful substance that can be used against many deadly diseases, or alternatively can be used to restore 10 ENDURANCE points if swallowed after combat. If you wish to keep the Potion, mark it on your *Action Chart* as a Backpack

3

Item. You should also restore the COMBAT SKILL points that were temporarily lost due to Limbdeath.

After dragging the dead Elix into the strongroom, you lock the steel door from the inside. You notice that there are in fact two doors to the strongroom: the one by which you entered, and a smaller door set into the opposite wall. The Gold Key opens the lock of the new door, which leads to a narrow staircase beyond, dimly lit by flaring torches in wall brackets.

The climb is steep and arduous. You suspect that these steps are part of a secret route to the strongroom, and your suspicions are only confirmed when you arrive at what appears to be a dead end. A closer examination reveals a narrow bronze door set flush to the wall, plain in appearance except for a tiny keyhole close to the floor. As you insert and twist the Gold Key, you are quietly confident that the bronze door will open.

Turn to **67**.

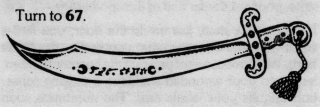

3

You search the bodies of the three vestibule guards and uncover the following items:

        4 Gold Crowns
        1 Dagger
        1 Sword

> 1 Potion of Alether (Increases your COMBAT SKILL by 2 points for the duration of one fight.)

You may also take the Blowpipe and the remaining Sleep Dart. If you decide to take them, mark them on your *Action Chart* as Backpack Items. In the robe of the dead blowpipe warrior, you find a small piece of parchment upon which is written today's date and the number sixty-seven.

A smile creeps across your face as you realize that this is the number that will open the bronze door. You hold your breath and twist the dial.

Turn to **67**.

4

You stoop to grasp the sword, but as your fingers close around the hilt, the second guard attacks.

Palace Jailer: COMBAT SKILL 14   ENDURANCE 21

Ignore all ENDURANCE points lost by the enemy in the first round of combat, for you can only attempt to parry his blow.

> If you win and the fight lasts for 4 rounds of combat or less, turn to **165**.
> If the fight lasts longer than 4 rounds of combat, turn to **180**.

5

You are half-way round the tower when a section of the sandstone ledge suddenly gives way beneath your feet. Desperately you claw at the masonry, but the stone is old and disintegrates in your hands. You topple backwards and fall to your doom in the palace gardens below.

Your escape and your life end here.

6

The oil is made from the fruit of the larnuma tree. It has a soothing and relaxing effect when rubbed into the skin.

> If you choose to rub the larnuma oil into your skin, turn to **103**.
>
> If you decide not to use the oil, turn to **71**.

7

You release the bowstring and the arrow arcs through the air towards your target. However, you have mis-judged the range and it falls short and shatters on the cobblestones of the harbour square, alerting Maouk's men to your whereabouts. You prepare to take flight, but the small boat is quickly surrounded and you are forced to surrender.

As the black-clad Sharnazim drag you along the harbour wall, you fear that your life is about to come to a sudden end.

Turn to **176**.

8

You channel all your Kai skill into detecting the number that will open the door; it is a strenuous task, and one that demands great concentration. Gradually, the image of two numbers – six and seven – begin to form in your mind. The image is hazy, and you are not sure if the number is sixty-seven or seventy-six. You are exhausted by your efforts and they have cost you 2 ENDURANCE points. Deduct these from your current ENDURANCE points total before choosing between the two possibilities.

If you decide to choose sixty-seven, turn to **67**.
If you decide to choose seventy-six, turn to **76**.

9

The guard begins to cough. He pleads with you to slacken your grip or he will choke to death. You ask him one more question: does he know where your confiscated equipment is? He says he does not know. Then, suddenly, he elbows you in the chest and breaks free. You are winded, but you are determined to stop him from escaping.

Turn to **78**.

10

The Sharnazim surround you and drag you to your feet. They take your Backpack, your Weapons, your Gold Crowns and *all* your Special Items. (Make all the necessary adjustments to your *Action Chart*.) Your hands are tied with wire and you are frog-marched back to the plaza. A carriage is waiting. As you are thrown in head first, Maouk climbs aboard and, gloating with triumph, gives the command:

'Back to the Grand Palace. The Zakhan awaits his prize.'

You struggle to free yourself from the wire that cuts into your wrists, but Maouk is quick to see the danger. He grabs your arm and forces a dart into your skin. As sleep numbs all your senses, the last sound you hear is Maouk's wicked laughter.

Turn to **69**.

11

To reach the north door without being seen, you must work your way carefully around the chamber, dodging from one pillar to the next.

Pick a number from the *Random Number Table*. If you possess the Kai Discipline of Camouflage or Hunting, deduct 2 from the number you have picked.

If your total is now −2–2, turn to **167**.
If your total is now 3 – 9, turn to **190**.

12 – *Illustration I*

You are in underwater combat with a deadly salt water scavenger.

Bloodlug: COMBAT SKILL 17   ENDURANCE 11

Deduct 2 points from your COMBAT SKILL due to the speed of its attack. This creature is immune to Mindblast.

If you win the fight, turn to **95**.

I. You are in underwater combat with a deadly salt water
scavenger

13

You force yourself along the canal, which is thick with green and black scum, clotted with a hideous variety of filth and debris. Huge cockroaches crawl in and out of the cracked ceiling. The vile water is waist deep, and as the surface scum breaks, a cloud of putrid gas wafts up and engulfs you. The stench is appalling, and choking, you cover your mouth and nose with the edge of your Kai cloak. A sudden splash warns you that Maouk's men are not far behind so you quicken your step.

You have waded only a few yards when you hear a soft rustling noise. You freeze. It is the unmistakable sound of scaled skin slithering softly over stone. Fear turns to blind terror as you catch your first glimpse of the creature now advancing towards you.

If you have the Kai Discipline of Animal Kinship, turn to **187**.
If you do not possess this skill, turn to **110**.

14

You step into a perfect hemisphere. The walls of the chamber curve smoothly into the ceiling, where a small window casts a splash of light across the floor. There is a large circular dais in the centre of the room laden with incense burners, decanters, quills, scrolls, cloaks, urns and all kinds of fruit and sweetmeats. A drawer catches your eye, protruding from beneath the lip of the dais; you recognize the contents. You have found your confiscated equipment. Restore to your *Action Chart* all the Backpack Items, Special Items, Weapons and Gold Crowns you lost when you were imprisoned.

Elated by your discovery, you resolve to escape from the Grand Palace as quickly as possible. There is only one other door, apart from the one by which you entered the chamber, which is set into the north wall.

If you wish to leave the chamber, turn to **58**.

If you wish to search the chamber for useful items, turn to **131**.

15

The tunnel is dark and shadowy. Much of it is in a poor state of repair, and many cracks and fissures scar the walls. You must search for one large enough in which to hide. Pick a number from the *Random Number Table*. If you have reached the Kai rank of Guardian or higher, deduct 1 from the number you have picked.

If your total is now *–1–7*, turn to **151**.

If your total is now *8–9*, turn to **175**.

16

You rush into the cellar and bolt the door. Pressing your ear to the gnarled timber, you listen intently to the noise of Maouk's angry soldiers. They have entered the building and it will only be a matter of time before they notice the cellar door. You cast your eyes around the room. It is empty except for a Coil of Rope and a Tinderbox. Then you notice that there is another way out of the small stone room – an iron grille in the centre of the floor. However, the horrible stench rising from it turns your stomach.

If you wish to leave the cellar by the grille, turn to **51**.

If you decide to stay in the cellar, prepare for combat and turn to **123**.

17

It takes a long time for the fear and nausea to subside but you push on through the slimy water, almost oblivious to your dreadful surroundings. Eventually you reach a junction where a wider tunnel crosses your path.

If you wish to continue along the west channel, turn to **73**.

If you wish to turn north into the new tunnel, turn to **112**.

If you wish to go south along the new tunnel, turn to **128**.

If you possess the Kai Discipline of Sixth Sense, turn to **47**.

18

The cell door does not open again until the sun has dipped below the peaks of the Dahir mountains. You prepare yourself to meet the Zakhan, to demand your immediate release and safe passage back to

Sommerlund, but it is not only the Zakhan who awaits you in the Grand Hall. He has a guest who has travelled many miles for this special meeting. His name is Haakon. He is a Darklord of Helgedad.

Unarmed and helpless, you are forced to kneel before the Darklord. With wicked relish, Haakon squeezes the life from your body with his own hands.

Your life and all hopes for your country end here.

19

You raise the hood of your Kai cloak in order to keep your face in shadow as you approach the guards. They eye you suspiciously, but are obviously reassured by your mastery of their language. You pretend to be a merchant whose goods have been confiscated and ask to be allowed to plead your case to the Judicar of Barrakeesh. The guards chuckle to themselves, and then demand two items from your Backpack before they allow you into the Grand Palace. They wink at each other, for they know that the Judicar never returns confiscated cargoes. They think you will be thrown in the palace cells for your insolence, like every other aggrieved merchant who has tried to plead for justice.

If you wish to give the guards what they demand,
erase any two Backpack Items (except Meals)
from your *Action Chart*. You may now pass
through the gate and enter the palace gardens.
Turn to **137**.

If you do not or cannot give the guards two Backpack Items, you must leave the gate and search
for some other means of entering the palace.
Turn to **49**.

20 – *Illustration II*

Frantically the warrior pulls on the reins, and tries to
trample you beneath the hooves of his startled horse.

Horseman: COMBAT SKILL 21   ENDURANCE 28

If you wish to evade combat at any time by jump-
ing into the sea, turn to **142**.

If you wish to evade combat by surrendering, turn
to **176**.

If you win the combat in three rounds or less, turn
to **125**.

If the fight lasts longer than three rounds, turn to
82.

If you lose the combat, turn to **161**.

21

Your lightning-fast reactions have saved you from
being hit. You dive forward and roll, so that the
needle pierces your cloak but not your skin. However, the trident-armed guards close in, confident
that the needle has found its mark and you are tran-
quillized. The instant they lower their weapons you
attack.

Turn to **168**.

II. The warrior tries to trample   you beneath the hooves of his
startled horse

22

You have sustained a deep chest wound that has penetrated your right lung. Lose 8 ENDURANCE points.

If you are still alive and possess the Kai Discipline of Healing, turn to **107**.

If you do not possess this skill, turn to **63**.

23

The climb would be easy if it were not for the scalding steam. It stings your face and hands, making the skin puffed and sore. Lose 1 ENDURANCE point.

Pick a number from the *Random Number Table*. If you have lost the use of one arm, deduct 3 points from the number you have picked. If you possess the Kai Discipline of Hunting, add 2 points to your total.

If your total is now *−3−−1*, turn to **77**.

If your total is now *0–6*, turn to **192**.

If your total is now *7–11*, turn to **114**.

24

The man slams the gate and draws the bolt. Seconds later you hear the footfalls of the Sharnazim as they rush into the courtyard. 'Go inside,' whispers the man, pointing to the darkened interior of his house. 'I shall get rid of the soldiers.'

You enter the house and climb a staircase to a large airy room, which looks out over a market-place. Long, black flags hang from the windows of a hall opposite, and the sounds of mourning can be heard through its open doors.

If you have the Kai Discipline of Sixth Sense, turn to **147**.
If you do not possess this skill, turn to **196**.

25

The dart sinks into your chest. You pull it free but a wave of nausea makes you fall to your knees. The tip of the missile is drugged and you cannot fight the darkness that now engulfs your vision.

Turn to **69**.

26

Peering through the keyhole, you can see that the lock is unusual; a small metal plate blocks the mechanism, so that it is impossible to pick the lock.

If you have the Kai Discipline of Mind Over Matter, turn to **48**.
If you wish to try to break down the door, turn to **127**.
If you decide to leave the door and head off along the other passage towards the stairs, turn to **93**.

27

Each of the three bottles bear a label, handwritten in green ink.

Larnuma oil (restores 2 ENDURANCE points per dose)
– 3 Gold Crowns

Laumspur (restores 4 ENDURANCE points per dose)
– 5 Gold Crowns

Rendalim's Elixir (restores 6 ENDURANCE points
per dose)– 7 Gold Crowns

You may purchase any of the above. (The prices are per dose. All the potions are Backpack Items.) The herb-mistress then escorts you to a side door. 'I sense your despair, Northlander. I pray you find your cure.'

As you leave, she offers a word of advice. 'The guards at the north gate of the Grand Palace can be bribed.' You thank her and enter the alley running along the side of her shop.

Turn to **160**.

28

The plan works – your arrow cuts the air and finds its mark. The smash of glass echoes around the square, drawing everyone's attention to the merchant's shop.

Turn to **153**.

29

After tying a large knot in one end of the rope, you gather the coils and hurl the knotted end towards your target. After three failures, your fourth attempt is successful; the knot jams in a V-shaped joint and you are able to pull yourself out of the water, and swing across the vault to jump safely into the opposite tunnel. However, you cross this obstacle at the cost of your rope; it still hangs from the metal bar and there is no way you can rescue it. (Remember to strike this item from your *Action Chart*.)

The passage ahead winds and curves like a giant snake, and the foul air wafting towards you is hot and humid. Although you seem to have shaken off your pursuers, you have yet to escape from the Baga-darooz.

Turn to **55**.

30

You pass several high-arched portals overlooking the east city wall, and continue easily and safely until you hear noises drifting along the passage. The voices of hungry guards and the distinctive clatter of plates and mugs warn you that a crowded mess hall lies ahead.

You are trying to decide on the best course of action , when a patrol of guards suddenly appears behind you in the corridor. Quickly, you jump on to a window ledge and take cover behind the arch of a portal. However, the arch is narrow and you are sure to be seen when the guards march past.

If you wish to hide outside on the narrow ledge that runs round the palace wall, turn to **152**.

If you wish to attack the guards as they march past, turn to **124**.

(continued over)

If you have reached the Kai rank of Guardian or
higher, turn to **62**.

31

As you start to climb, two Sharnazim warriors suddenly emerge from the insect-choked tunnel. They
lunge at you, their hands outstretched, their fingers
hooked to claw at your legs and drag you down. You
kick out and strike one of the cruel-faced men
beneath the jaw. He clutches at his throat and gives a
gurgling cry as he falls backwards into the slimy water.

You reach the stone trapdoor, but the other warrior
has unsheathed his scimitar and has begun to climb
the ladder; he no longer intends to capture you alive.
Pressing your shoulder to the cobwebbed trapdoor,
you push up the heavy stone and scramble out to find
yourself in a noisy alley, crowded with people and
market stalls. The sewer hole itself is close to a wicker
table stacked high with bundles of torches.

If you possess a Kalte Firesphere or a Tinderbox,
turn to **143**.
If you do not have either of these Items, turn to
183.

32

You raise the hood of your cloak and hurry through
the open doors into the dark, cool hall. The people
are kneeling in front of a pulpit where a holy man,
dressed in flowing robes of black and gold, reads
aloud from a gem-encrusted book. Behind him, the
face of the late Zakhan, immortalized in a tapestry
suspended from the roof by huge silken cords, looks
down on the mourners.

The congregation is wrapped in prayer and nobody sees you enter. The ceremony soon comes to an end and you are able to slip past Maouk's men as the mourners flood into the streets.

Turn to **169**.

33

You hack the dirt-encrusted floor and uncover a large metal ring, which proves to be part of an old trap-door. The metal ring is badly corroded but you manage to prise the trapdoor open. It covers a deep shaft; from the inky darkness below comes the stench of the sewer.

The Sharnazim are climbing up the stone steps. Their pounding footsteps match your racing heartbeat.

If you wish to jump down the shaft, turn to **94**.
If you wish to stand and fight the Sharnazim, turn to **185**.

34

No matter how hard you try to picture the mechanism in your mind's eye, the image will not appear. Deduct 1 ENDURANCE point due to the strain of your mental exertion.

If you want to try to break down the door, turn to
127.

If you decide to leave the door and head off along
the other passage towards the stairs, turn to **93**.

35

The great snake shudders and convulses in the throes
of death. The smell of its thick brown blood is disgusting and you have to hold your breath and grit your
teeth as you lift the dead Yas away from the chest and
peer inside.

You discover six, silver-handled maces, each beautifully carved and encrusted with rubies, emeralds and
pearls. In the Northlands these weapons would fetch
thousands of crowns. At the bottom of the chest, you
also discover a small Copper Key. If you wish to take
either a Jewelled Mace or the Copper Key, or both,
mark them on your *Action Chart* as Special Items.
You carry the Copper Key in the pocket of your tunic,
and the Jewelled Mace tucked into your belt.

The acidic smell of the snake blood is beginning to
make you retch. Quickly, you climb the stone steps
and leave the armoury by the north door.

Turn to **14**.

36

The grim-faced Sharnazim encircle you, their razor-
sharp scimitars glinting in the afternoon sun. 'Take
him!' shouts Maouk. 'But take him alive!'

Reluctantly, the warriors sheathe their swords and
wait for a chance to rush you. Six lie dead at your feet
before you are eventually overpowered. 'You are

brave, Kai Lord,' says Maouk, in a mocking tone,
'but you will need more than bravery to save you
now.'

Turn to **176**.

37

The Imperial Apothecary can only be reached from
the palace gardens by entering the Vizu-diar. The
kitchens are part of the slaves quarters, under
constant supervision of the cruel slave-masters and
guards. You wait until the path and lawns are
deserted before you run across to the door of the
Vizu-diar.

Turn to **149**.

38

Half-way round the small tower, a section of the sandstone ledge begins to crumble beneath your feet.
Instinctively, you leap sideways and stretch out your
hands in time to grasp the firm ledge beyond. The
drop below is terrifying, but your terror gives you the
impetus and strength you need to claw your way
back on to the ledge. Your fingers are bleeding and

bruised, but you are still alive. You lose 1 ENDURANCE point.

Turn to **87**.

39

The man is lying. He knows that other guards are sure to turn up at any moment. As soon as you loosen your grip, he will attempt to overpower you and raise the alarm.

If you wish to continue questioning him, turn to **9**.

If you decide to kill him, turn to **78**.

40

The Kwaraz drops from the ceiling and plunges into the water, creating an enormous wave of foul slime which completely submerges you. Wracked with nausea, you cough and retch, and try to scoop the muck from your eyes and mouth. The Kwaraz's carcass blocks the tunnel and you can only get past by climbing over it. Still in a state of shock, you lose 1 Backpack Item, your pouch of Gold Crowns and 2 ENDURANCE points. Make the necessary adjustments to your *Action Chart*.

If you are still alive, turn to **17**.

41

You fill your mouth with oil but cannot bring yourself to swallow it – the foul tasting liquid makes you feel sick. You spit it out, and gulp mouthfuls of water to rid yourself of the disgusting taste.

If you now decide to rub some of the oil into your skin, turn to **103**.

If you decide to forget the vile-tasting oil completely, turn to **71**.

42

Your Kai sense warns you that the alley is a dead end. If you take that exit from the square, you will certainly be trapped. Only two other choices remain: the high, nail-studded gate to your left, or the path directly ahead.

If you decide to go through the gate, turn to **75**.
If you decide to take the path, turn to **169**.

43

You reach a small chamber set above the tunnel. Here, at least, it is dry, although the foul sewer gas permeates everything. You hurry along a narrow passage, which turns first to the west and then to the south, but your heart sinks as you see a dead end looming out of the inky blackness.

If you wish to search for a hidden exit, turn to **33**.
If you wish to prepare yourself for combat, turn to **185**.

44

You hurry through the west door and into the welcoming cool of the corridor beyond. A large drawbar on the inside of the door catches your eye; you lock it to delay any would-be pursuers.

At the end of the corridor lies a hall full of weapons. Racks of spears and swords line the chamber walls, and a massive workbench covers the floor. It is the palace armoury. In the midst of the tools which litter the workbench, there is a large, black, leatherbound book.

If you wish to examine the book, turn to **83**.
If you wish to ignore the book and search for your confiscated equipment instead, turn to **181**.

45

You concentrate your Mindblast on the guard's hand. He screams and his fingers spring open as his hand is robbed of all feeling and control. He is now unarmed.

If you wish to attack the guard, turn to **78**.
If you wish simply to overpower him and capture him alive, turn to **199**.

46

As your adversary falls to the ground, the other guard stabs at you with his trident. You cannot evade combat and must fight him to the death.

Vestibule Guard 2:
COMBAT SKILL 14   ENDURANCE 24

If you win the combat, turn to **3**.

47

You have a strong feeling that more Kwaraz occupy the north tunnel. You sense a lair. It would be almost suicide to go that way, so you must take one of the remaining routes.

If you wish to continue along the west tunnel, turn to **73**.

If you wish to go south along the new tunnel, turn to **128**.

48

You focus on the lock and concentrate all of your Kai skill on opening it. Sweat begins to trickle down your face. Pick a number from the *Random Number Table*. If you have reached the Kai rank of Guardian or higher, add 3 to the number you have picked.

If you total is now *0–4*, turn to **34**.

If your total is now 5 or higher, turn to **80**.

49

The outer wall of the Grand Palace is far too high to climb; and even if you had a rope long enough, your green Kai cloak would be seen for miles, set against the white, sun-bleached marble wall.

You crouch in the shadow of a doorway while you concentrate on working out a plan. There is a constant traffic of mounted scouts and couriers from the north gate. Those arriving hand a scroll of parchment to two of the guards before they enter. Slowly, a bold plan begins to take shape in your mind. If you could overpower one of the couriers before he reaches the palace gate, you could disguise yourself in his clothes and use his scroll to gain entrance.

50

Many of the couriers approach the Grand Palace from the harbour, and although it is infested with troops you discover the ideal place to ambush a rider. There is a broad avenue where a bridge of gnarled wood and metal curves over the street, and here, beneath the wooden arch, you lie in wait for your prey.

Your chance soon arrives; a black-robed rider enters the avenue and spurs his horse along the street. He will have to pass beneath the arch. You prepare to pounce.

Pick a number from the *Random Number Table*. If you have the Kai Discipline of Hunting, add 1 to the number you have picked. If you have reached the Kai rank of Savant, add 3 to the number you have picked.

If your total is now *0–5*, turn to **106**.
If your total is now *6–13*, turn to **189**.

50

The smooth leather soles of your boots do not grip on the wet wood. You slip, and as you fall you gash your head on the row of oars. You lose 2 ENDURANCE points.

You are fished from the water by the Sharnazim; they drag you by your cloak across the sun-bleached flag-stones of the harbour square and deposit you at Maouk's feet. He looks at you mockingly. 'You are brave, Kai Lord. But you will need more than bravery to save you now.'

Turn to **176**.

51

A slippery ladder disappears into the dark, stench-filled shaft. You gulp a lungful of air and climb down, locking the trapdoor behind you. When you finally reach the bottom of the shaft, your worst fears are confirmed.

You have entered the Baga-darooz, the main drainage sewer of Barrakeesh. You recall one of the crewmen aboard the galley, an old man nicknamed 'The Stink' because he smelt so much, having been sentenced to one year's imprisonment in the Baga-darooz for a crime he did not commit. Peering along the gloomy tunnels, you wonder how he survived for so long in this dank, filthy sewer.

Suddenly your thoughts are disturbed by the sound of splintering wood. Chunks of shattered timber rain down upon you as the Sharnazim force open the trapdoor. The heavy iron grille glances off your shoulder as it falls; you stifle your cry of pain but you lose 1 ENDURANCE point due to the wound.

This section of the Baga-darooz is a junction where three channels meet. You must quickly decide which channel to take, for Maouk's men are now descending the ladder.

> If you have the Kai Discipline of Tracking, turn to **173**.
> If you wish to enter the left channel, turn to **96**.
> If you wish to enter the right channel, turn to **145**.
> If you wish to enter the channel straight ahead, turn to **13**.

52

You turn the body over with the toe of your boot and search the robes, discovering the following items:

> 4 Gold Crowns
> Jailer's Keys (Special Item)
> Dagger
> Sword

If you wish to keep any of these items, remember to mark them on your *Action Chart*. (The Jailer's Keys should be worn on your belt.)

Turn to **140**.

53

You recognize the sign of the fish. It is the symbol of a holy order of monks known as 'The Redeemers', a silent order who are devoted to a lifetime of prayer, pilgrimage, and the study of the healing arts.

If you wish to enter the dwelling, turn to **157**.

If you decide to enter the tavern instead, turn to **188**.

54 – *Illustration III*

Hurrying down the steps and away from the Bath Hall, you enter the 'Saadi-tas-Ouda': the Square of the Dead. Jet-black flagstones cover the square, each with a long iron spike set deep into its centre. From the Bath Hall steps, the square resembles the back of a massive iron porcupine, but when you reach the base of the steps, you realize that the Saddi-tas-Ouda is in fact far more sinister.

Stuck on top of each spike is a human skull – all that

III.   Impaled upon the sharp iron pole is the head of the
Vassagonian envoy

remains of pirates, murderers, traitors and thieves who have been sentenced to death. The grisly display serves as a warning to others never to defy the law of the Zakhan.

As you reach the far side of the square, you brush against a spike. Fresh blood is smeared across the arm of your tunic, staining it dark red. You raise your eyes, cursing at your misfortune, but you are shocked into silence by the sight before you.

Impaled upon the sharp iron pole is the head of the Vassagonian envoy. To either side are the heads of all the galley crew. On each of their foreheads is freshly branded one word – TRAITOR. Fear wells up inside you; turning your face away from their sightless eyes, you run into the crowded streets of the Mikarum, the district where the spice and herb merchants live.

At the end of a narrow, winding street, you reach a junction. Opposite is a shop with a bright red sign above the door:

Bir Dar Masoun
HERB-MISTRESS

If you need the Oede herb, turn to **68**.
If you do not need this herb, but still decide to enter the shop, turn to **154**.
If you wish to continue along a new alleyway that heads off towards the Grand Palace, turn to **179**.

55

The temperature rises steadily until you are bathed in sweat. Ahead, you see a chamber filled with steam that rises from its bubbling floor. You are about to enter the chamber when you catch a glimpse of the danger awaiting you; the stone walkway ends abruptly, only a few yards into the chamber. Ten feet below, lying before you like the surface of a huge, bubbling cauldron, is a tar-sorkh: a mud geyser.

These geysers are common in Vassagonia. Much of the desert empire is unstable, but although it is subject to constant earth tremors, it rarely results in great destruction. The Vassagonians call these tremors: 'Tasa-Dophiem', which means 'The Wrestling Gods'.

This particular mud geyser has been put to practical use. It provides a constant source of heat for the dwellings built over the chamber. The steam from the tar-sorkh rises into a pair of huge, circular chimneys in the domed ceiling, which in turn feed heat to the buildings above. Your only way out of this chamber is by climbing one of these chimneys. Although there are no ladders, the rock-hewn chamber wall offers many footholds.

If you wish to climb the left chimney, turn to **162**.
If you wish to climb the right chimney, turn to **23**.

56

A search of the baskets crowding the little boat uncovers a beautifully hand-tooled leather case. You flick open the brass catch and discover that the case contains a Jakan – a hunting bow used by the coastal fishermen of Vassagonia. You are elated by the find but disappointed to discover that the case contains only one arrow.

57

Across the harbour square, close to Maouk's carriage, you notice a small, white-walled shop where a row of green glass flagons line a balcony on the first floor. You draw the bowstring to your lips and take careful aim; it is a difficult shot and you have only one chance.

Pick a number from the *Random Number Table*. If you possess the Kai Discipline of Weaponskill (any weapon), add 2 to the number you have picked.

If your total is now *0–3*, turn to **7**.
If your total is now *4–11*, turn to **28**.

57

The door is unlocked and for a moment your heart sinks; if this room is the Imperial Apothecary where the Oede herb is kept, why is the door not locked and guarded? Anxiously you slip inside and survey the interior.

It seems to be an apothecary. Glass retorts bubble and steam over jets of blue flame, and strange fluids pass back and forth through a crazy maze of tubes and funnels. Hundreds of herb jars line the far wall, and ten large copper urns, each full of rainbow-coloured powder, hang suspended from the soot-blackened ceiling. You begin searching through the herb jars, and suddenly you discover why the door was left unlocked. Creeping slowly towards you is the cat-like creature that guards the apothecary. Its eyes glow with a vivid green luminescence as it prepares to strike.

Elix: COMBAT SKILL 17 ENDURANCE 32

If you have ever fought an Elix before, add 2 to your COMBAT SKILL for the duration of this fight. You cannot evade the combat and must fight it to the death.

If you win the combat, turn to **2**.

58

You follow a straight passage of pale, rose-coloured stone, which soon ends at an empty vestibule. In its north wall is set a great wooden door, covered with engraved bronze plaques and studded with bronze nails. There is a curious lock set into the middle of this door, encircled by a beautiful carving of a long-tailed scorpion. A closer look at the lock reveals a series of Vassagonian numerals, numbered 1 to 200, engraved in the lock. You recognize the design: it is a Cloeasian combination lock.

If you know the correct number that will open the bronze door, turn to that section number.

If you do not know the number that will open the door, turn to **156**.

59

You spring forward and slam your fist into the guard's face; he grunts and falls, clutching a bleeding nose. His sword drops to the ground close by your feet.

If you wish to pick up the sword, turn to **4**.

If you wish to ignore the sword and attack the second guard with your bare hands, turn to **91**.

60

You leap towards the first warrior, feigning a blow that makes him dodge to the left. You anticipate his move and catch him in mid-step. He doubles up and then crumples into the slimy water, clutching his wound. The others hesitate and then back away.

Suddenly a voice echoes along the tunnel. 'Leave him to me, you fools!' Maouk appears from the shadows, a dart held high in his hand. He hisses a curse and flings the missile at your chest.

Turn to **25**.

61

Suddenly, the door bursts open and in rush the Sharnazim. You make a dash for the open window, but are grabbed from behind and pulled to the ground. Lashing out with your feet and fists you free yourself, only to be overpowered by more of the dark-skinned warriors. As they drag you out into the courtyard, you catch a glimpse of the man who opened the gate; he smiles at you as he slips a pouch of silver into his pocket.

Turn to **176**.

62

Instinct and experience warn you that it would be rash to attack the guards so close to a crowded mess hall; any noise of combat would immediately be heard by the soldiers inside. There is now only one course of action for you to take – you must hide outside on the ledge running round the palace wall.

Turn to **152**.

63

You tear strips of cloth from your Kai cloak and bandage the wound as best you can. You manage to staunch the flow, but you have lost a lot of blood and fear the wound is infected.

Deduct 2 ENDURANCE points from your total, for every section of the book through which you pass, until you discover and swallow a potion of Laumspur. If your ENDURANCE points total falls to 0 before you discover the healing potion, you will die from blood poisoning.

If you wish to search the bodies of the dead guards, turn to **102**.

If you wish to ignore the bodies and escape along the corridor, turn to **150**.

64 – *Illustration IV (overleaf)*

You have barely taken a dozen steps along the walkway when you hear a low, inhuman growl. Then, the noise suddenly changes to an abominable and high-pitched sputter, as the huge bulk of a Kwaraz emerges from out of the dark. It is upon you before you can take any evasive action.

Kwaraz: COMBAT SKILL 20   ENDURANCE 30

The giant reptile is very susceptible to psychic power. If you have the Kai Discipline of Mindblast, add 4 (instead of the normal 2) to your COMBAT SKILL for the duration of the combat.

If you win the combat, turn to **177**.

IV. The huge bulk of a Kwaraz emerges from out of the dark

65

The guard slumps to the ground, his neck broken by the blow from the edge of your hand, but as you turn you see that the other man has recovered from your punch and is crawling across the floor, his hand stretched out to retrieve his sword.

If you wish to attack the guard, turn to **78**.

If you wish simply to overpower him and capture him alive, turn to **199**.

66

A sour-faced guard with a whip stands at the great doors to the kitchen. He delights in bullying the slaves that pass to and fro, lashing them with his whip and cursing them foully. You decide it is far too risky to confront the guard, and instead focus your attention on the kitchen windows. The guard is too engrossed in beating an unfortunate slave who has dropped a basket of fruit to notice you sprint across the gardens and leap into the shadow of a tall, arched kitchen window. Then, to your horror, you notice that two guards are seated inside the kitchen, just below the window ledge on which you now stand. If they should so much as turn their heads, you will be seen.

If you wish to jump back into the palace gardens and try to enter the palace through the Zakhan's trophy room, turn to **149**.

If you wish to launch a surprise attack on the seated guards, before they notice you are there, turn to **124**.

67

You hear a faint click followed by a soft whirring

sound; the bronze door slides open. As you hurry through, the door clicks shut behind your back, as softly as it had opened.

Instinct tells you that you have entered the chambers of the upper palace, the sumptuous private enclave of the Zakhan. You walk upon glistening tiles of opal and platinum, past sculptures and statues of pure gold. The door of solid amethyst ahead seems plain in comparison to the breathtaking splendour of this private world. Beyond the door lies another unique and startlingly beautiful world: the arboretum. A circular, cathedral-like arena spreads out below you, a green velvet canopy alive with the sound of bird-song. Trees of every colour, shape and size flourish in the deep dark soil of the floor. The Zakhan's arboretum houses a specimen of every tree that grows in Magnamund, and many species that are now extinct. As you walk the wrought iron balcony which encircles the arboretum, you recognize the leaves of a Sommlending oak. You feel a sudden wave of homesickness, but it does not make you despair; rather it renews your determination to escape from this hostile, sun-bleached land.

At one of the exits from the arboretum, you discover a Quarterstaff propped against the wall. (If you wish to take this, remember to mark it on your *Action Chart*.) The desire to escape urges you on as you leave the arboretum and hurry through a network of lavish corridors and empty, deserted vestibules. You reach a landing where a broad staircase descends to a massive room that occupies most of the lower palace.

From the top of the staircase, hidden by the shadow

of a pilaster, you stare down on a sight that freezes
your blood with terror.

Turn to **200**.

68

You part the curtain of beads hanging in the doorway
and enter the cool interior. The lifeless arm that hangs
limply by your side has taken on a bluish hue. Fear
returns; you must find the Oede herb to cure the
disease, or you will lose the whole limb and possibly
your life.

A woman appears from the shadows of the counter.
She has piercing green eyes and her red hair is raised,
bound round with rings of jadin. 'Welcome Northlander,' she says, in a voice both soft and clear. 'How
may I serve you?'

You hesitate before replying, 'Oede.'

She narrows her eyes and casts a glance at your
injured arm. 'I cannot help you,' she says sorrowfully.
'Oede is now a very rare and precious herb. I would

have to sell my shop and all my possessions in order to buy just one small pouch of Oede. There is only one man in Barrakeesh rich enough to possess this herb – the Zakhan.'

Sweat breaks out upon your brow as your fear grows. 'What little Oede there is,' she continues, 'is kept in the Grand Palace under lock and key.'

You ask if there is any other herb that can cure your arm. She shakes her head from side to side. 'Only Oede will cure Limbdeath – and you can only find that in the strongroom of the Imperial Apothecary.' She reaches behind the counter and brings forward three glass bottles, each containing a coloured liquid. 'They will not cure you, but they will dull the pain in the last few hours.'

If you wish to examine the potions, turn to **27**.
If you decide to ignore them, leave the shop and continue along the alley, turn to **160**.

69

You wake up in great discomfort; every muscle of your body feels knotted and bruised. You force open eyelids clogged with dried sweat, and look with dread at your wretched surroundings. You are lying on the hard stone floor of a prison cell. Over by the far wall, beneath a window crisscrossed with iron bars, is a low wooden bunk covered in filthy rags. Cockroaches, some the size of field mice, scuttle along a foul-smelling gutter that disappears into a grating in the floor.

You discover that your hands are free, and slowly pull yourself upright into a sitting position, resting your back against the cell door. A faint draught from the corridor outside provides the only relief from the stifling heat and bad air of the cell. In the distance, you can hear footsteps approaching. Then there is a jangle of keys and the creak of hinges. A door closes with a dull thud. More footsteps; they are getting louder. They come to a halt outside the cell door and a loud voice bellows out: 'Sleeping on duty, Sefrou? You'll wake up on the other side of this door if the captain catches you!'

A chair scrapes along the ground, and a startled voice, full of indignation, replies: 'Curse you, Hadj! The Zakhan doesn't want the Northlander taken to the Grand Hall until sunset. You've cheated me of two hours sleep.'

'Shut up, Sefrou,' snarls the first voice, 'and listen hard. I've just come from the armoury. Some interesting trinkets were found on the Northlander, worth a great deal of gold I'd say. Seems a pity to let them go to waste, eh?'

70

The two guards chuckle greedily, and discuss at length the good time they will be able to have in the city, once they have sold your equipment.

'I'll take a peek at our friend,' says one of the guards. 'I wonder if he's enjoying our hospitality?'

A spy-hole slides open above your head and you hear a gasp of shock. 'He's gone! He's gone! By the Majhan, we'll lose our heads!' You suddenly realize that you cannot be seen so close to the door.

'Let me see,' hisses the other guard, eager to see for himself. You hear the click of a key in the lock; this could be your chance to escape.

If you wish to attack the guards as soon as the door opens, turn to **138**.

If you wish to move away from the door and stand in the middle of the cell, turn to **85**.

70

You press on for about a mile until you can go no further: a huge iron grating blocks the tunnel. The decomposing carcass of a giant lizard has been washed up against the bars. Bones are clearly visible where the dead flesh has rotted or been eaten away. The bars are firmly fixed; it will be impossible to continue in this direction.

Close to the dead lizard, a narrow stone platform juts out from the wall. Beyond the platform, you notice a low arch leading to some stairs, ascending out of the sewer.

The sound of Maouk's voice drifts along the tunnel. He is urging his Sharnazim in your direction.

If you wish to climb the steps, turn to **43**.

If you wish to wait here and fight your pursuers, turn to **60**.

71

Having washed off the worst of the dirt, you clamber out of the bath and enter a small antechamber; the room is hot and arid and your clothes are soon as dry as a bone. Beyond the antechamber is another hall, this time crowded with people, some seated, others standing, and everyone busy in conversation. These are the free baths of Barrakeesh and the citizens of the capital are justly proud of them. They are the envy of the other desert cities where water is scarce and precious. The citizens treat the baths as a forum, a place for meeting and talking with friends. Much of the conversation you overhear is about the new Zakhan; few speak well of him.

You wrap yourself in the large Towel and make your way through the crowd towards the main entrance. If you wish to keep the Towel once you are outside, you must mark it on your *Action Chart* as 2 Backpack Items, due to its size.

Turn to **54**.

72

'Go away!' shouts the plump landlady of this tavern. 'We've no hospitality for those who show no respect to our dead Zakhan.'

Two burly men, wearing wide arm-bands of black silk, roughly push you out of the tavern door. You slip and fall on the dusty cobblestones, grazing your hip and elbows. Lose 1 ENDURANCE point. As you get to your feet, Maouk and his warriors rush into the plaza and surround you.

If you wish to fight them, turn to **36**.
If you wish to surrender, turn to **176**.

73

The stench of the sewer begins to fade and the water becomes less polluted the further you explore in this direction. The sound of Maouk's men has faded and now only the constant gurgle and rush of the fetid water fills your ears. Suddenly your foot is caught by something and you are thrown off balance. Half-buried in the sludge of the tunnel floor is a rusty suit of armour.

Turn to **94**.

74

You detect that the west door leads to the palace armoury.

If you wish to go through the west door, turn to **44**.
If you wish to avoid the armoury, leave the chamber by the north door, and turn to **167**.

75

You twist the handle but the gate is locked. You are about to turn and run when suddenly the gate flies open: a man stands in the doorway. 'Quickly North-lander, I will hide you!' The man steps back to allow you to enter.

If you wish to enter, turn to **24**.
If you wish to refuse and climb the path towards the archway, turn to **169**.
If you wish to enter the alley, turn to **117**.

76

You flick the dial to 76 and press your shoulder against the great bronze plaques, expecting to hear at any moment the creak of hinges. You detect a sound, but it is not the noise of a door opening – you have chosen the wrong number.

Turn to **98**.

77

Your numb arm makes the climb impossible. Valiantly you struggle to escape up the chimney, but when a spur of rock breaks away in your hand, you cannot prevent yourself from tumbling backwards into the bubbling mud.

Your life comes to a swift end as you are boiled to death in the tar-sorkh of Barrakeesh.

78

Your attack is swift and deadly. Before the guard can scream for help, you have silenced him for good with an open-handed chop to the neck.

If you wish to leave the bodies and escape along the corridor, turn to **150**.
If you wish to search them, turn to **102**.

79

A line of toa trees casts a shadow that hides your stealthy approach. The iron portcullis is down, and only a couple of soldiers stand guard inside where there would normally be ten times that number. Suddenly, there is the grate of metal as the portcullis slowly rises. The guards stand back to allow a troop of cavalry to leave the palace. As they gallop past, the horses kick up a huge cloud of dust, covering the luckless guards from head to toe. They cough and sneeze and run to a horse-trough to slake their dust-choked throats. The portcullis is still open, the archway unguarded.

If you decide to attempt to sneak past the drinking guards, turn to **86**.

If you decide to attack them while their backs are turned, turn to **119**.

If you possess the Kai Disciplines of both Camouflage and Hunting, turn to **170**.

80

Within seconds, the image of the lock appears in your mind. You use your power to make the lock open and a loud 'click' confirms your success.

Turn to **136**.

81

You recognize the symptoms of Limbdeath. The wound has become infected by thousands of Limbdeath microbes, one of many strains of deadly bacteria to be found in the Baga-darooz. None of your Kai skills can prevent the eventual loss of your arm. There is only one cure for the disease – the infected wound must be treated with the herb Oede within twenty-four hours. Unless you find some Oede by mid-afternoon tomorrow, your arm will become gangrenous. You will then have to choose between losing your arm or losing your life.

This dreadful realization renews your determination to escape from this terrible place, for you can be sure of one thing: you will find no Oede in the Baga-darooz.

Turn to **166**.

82

You fight with great skill and courage but you are heavily outnumbered. The black-clad warriors close in and overpower you, dragging you back to a jubilant Maouk.

'You are brave, Kai Lord. But you will need more than bravery to save you now!'

Turn to **176**.

83

It is an armoury log. The pages contain handwritten lists of all the work carried out here. Spears and swords made for the garrison of Kara Kala, ore shipments from the Vakar mountains, weapons due for repair and all manner of daily routines are carefully recorded.

You are about to discard the log when you notice a folded piece of parchment tucked into the spine. It is a list of dates and numbers with a heading in bold print: '**The Bronze Door**'. You scan the page and locate today's date. The number listed next to it is '67'. Make a note of this number in the margin of your *Action Chart* – it could be of use at a later stage of your adventure.

You throw the book back on to the cluttered bench and begin to search for your missing equipment.

Turn to **181**.

84

You dive into the putrid water, steeling yourself for the ghastly swim you have decided to make. The oily scum fills your nose and mouth and chokes in your throat. You claw your way across the vault to the opposite tunnel and struggle on to a narrow walkway. You are trembling, but it is not the shock of the swim that has made you shiver. Your arm will not function. Your shoulder, wounded when the trapdoor grille fell, stings painfully, and the whole arm below it is numb and useless. Horror engulfs you as you realize what is wrong.

Turn to **81**.

85

The guards pull open the door and rush into the cell, their weapons held in readiness to attack. They are brutish men with cruel, war-scarred faces. Their surprise at your sudden appearance soon turns to anger and they shove you back against the far wall.

'Seems we have a trickster, Sefrou,' hisses the taller guard. 'A northland illusionist who's lost his way,' croons the other. They snigger at their joke, their eyes full of malevolence and spite.

'Let's teach our guest a lesson,' says the first guard, raising his blade to your throat. 'Go fetch the thumbscrews.'

> If you wish to attack the guard who holds the sword, turn to **59**.
> If you do not wish to attack, turn to **163**.

86

You sprint through the archway, keeping a watchful eye on the two drinking guards. The dust is settling; and should they turn round, you will certainly be seen. In your hurry, you fail to see a stone statue close to the wall and catch it with your knee. Stifling a yelp of pain, you hobble into the palace gardens and take cover beneath a leafy kasl bush. You lose 1 ENDURANCE point due to your injury, but at least you have entered the Grand Palace unseen.

Turn to **137**.

87

On the far side of the small tower, the ledge passes directly beneath a line of windows set high in the north wall. The sandstone blocks have been severely eroded by the strong ocean winds, creating many cracks and hollows which make climbing easy. To your delight, you also discover that the iron window grilles have yet to be locked on this side of the palace.

You drop to the floor of a corridor that heads off to

the west. A wide stairway leads up to a network of passages set with alcoves. Each alcove contains a bust or tapestry depicting past Zakhans, and Vassagonian victories in long-forgotten wars.

If you have the Kai Discipline of Sixth Sense, turn to **105**.
If you do not possess this skill, turn to **158**.

88

The poster is written from right to left in Vassagonian script. The time you spent learning the language aboard the galley was well spent, for you have little difficulty in translating the proclamation:

> His most illustrious majesty, Zakhan Moudalla the Exalted, has passed into the realm of the Majhan. May his spirit never die! By the grace of the Council of Kadi, the Funtal of Kara Kala and the Judicar of Barrakeesh, it is decreed that Kimah, Emir of Ferufezan, Protector of the Dry Main, shall by right claim the throne of Vassagonia. Through the unity of the Seven Cities, he will lead his people to greatness.

> Long may he reign!

A scuffle breaks out at the end of the passage as a handful of Sharnazim try to push their way through the crowd. In the confusion a fruit stall is overturned and its owner curses the clumsy soldiers at the top of his voice. There is a sudden silence– the luckless man has been beheaded for his insolence.

You turn and run, splashing through the shallow drainage channel running the length of the foul passage.

Turn to **113**.

89

A sharp pain stabs through your jaw as the needle finds its mark. In an instant, the room becomes a spinning vortex of darkness, beyond the reach of pain.

You awake to find yourself back in the cockroach-infested prison cell from which you originally escaped. You have been disarmed and stripped of all equipment, and can do little now except await the arrival of the Zakhan.

Turn to **18**.

90 – *Illustration V (overleaf)*

You enter a large vestibule constructed from blocks of pink and white marble. A man in a white robe sits near a door in the far wall; he is reading a scroll held close to his face. He has not seen you enter the baths, but he is quick to sense your presence.

'By the Majhan!' he cries. 'You smell worse than a Baknar!' He hurls a towel at you and points to the door. 'Take my advice,' he whines, his fingers

V.   A man in a white robe sits near a door in the far wall, reading
a scroll

pinching shut his nostrils. 'Don't get undressed – your clothes need the bath as much as you.'

You grit your teeth in anticipation of the moment when he sees that you are not Vassagonian, but he simply returns to his scroll, holding the parchment close to his short-sighted eyes. You smile as you realize that the man cannot see you clearly enough to know you are a foreigner.

Beyond the door there is a long hall, leading at regular intervals into smaller open chambers, each with a sunken bath. Perfumed water constantly splashes into the baths and drains away directly into the Baga-darooz. You decide to take the bath attendant's advice, and jump straight into the cool water keeping all your clothes on. You notice a large earthenware jar stands beside the bath, full to the brim with translucent purple oil.

If you have the Kai Discipline of Healing, turn to **6**.
If you wish to swallow some of the purple oil, turn to **41**.
If you wish to rub some into your skin, turn to **103**.
If you decide to ignore the oil, turn to **71**.

91

The guard lashes out at your head with his war-hammer. Instinctively, you duck, rolling to one side as the weapon strikes sparks from the wall.

Palace Jailer: COMBAT SKILL 14   ENDURANCE 21

You must deduct 4 points from your COMBAT SKILL for the duration of this combat, as you are without a weapon.

(continued over)

If you win and the fight lasts 4 rounds of combat or
less, turn to **65**.

If the fight lasts longer than 4 rounds of combat,
turn to **180**.

92

You sprint along the cobblestones but are soon
forced to stop. Cavalry appear at the end of the street;
they shout and charge at you, three abreast. Maouk
hisses a curse. You are shocked by how close his
voice sounds, as if he were but a step behind you.
You wheel round to confront him, only to see he still
stands where he first appeared. A dart is held high in
his hand; he hisses another curse and flings the
missile into the air.

Turn to **25**.

93

You descend the stairs and follow the corridor east-
wards, taking care to tread lightly. The bars on
windows high in the wall to your right cast latticed
shadows across the smooth marble floor ahead.
Beneath one of these windows stands a table on
which rests a pitcher of water. Your throat is parched
and you stop to take a long drink. Restore
1 ENDURANCE point.

If you wish to climb on to the table and look
through the window, turn to **155**.

If you wish to press on along the corridor, turn to
182.

94

You fall face first into putrid water. The oily slime fills

your ears and nose and chokes in your throat. You surface and struggle on to a narrow walkway, only to find that your arm no longer functions. Your wounded shoulder, injured by the falling trapdoor grille, still stings painfully, but now the whole arm below it is numb and useless. Horror overcomes you as you realize what is wrong.

Turn to **81**.

95

You surface beside a covered skiff. Anxious to avoid the scavengers in the waters of Barrakeesh harbour, you haul yourself aboard and hide beneath the boat's canopy of woven rushes. You are breathless from your swim but you dare not make a sound; Maouk's men are everywhere, racing along the harbour walls, their eyes searching the water for any sign of you. If you are to escape, you must think of something to divert their attention.

If you have the Kai Discipline of Mind Over Matter, turn to **184**.

If you do not possess this skill, turn to **56**.

96

The water is clotted with a revolting variety of green and black muck and scum. It reaches up to your waist, and, as you force your way through the glutinous mire, the surface film breaks, releasing a vile gas. You have to cover your nose and mouth with your Kai cloak, for the stench is appalling. A sudden splash warns that Maouk's men are not far behind.

Your foot catches in something buried in the silt of the

tunnel floor, and for one brief second, you are seized by total panic. You struggle to kick free but are held fast. Blindly, you stab your weapon beneath the filthy water until your foot is finally freed. As you withdraw your weapon, you half-expect to find some hideous sewer creature impaled upon it. Instead, you discover a human rib-cage. You shudder and flick the bones back into the stinking mire.

The channel soon divides: a new tunnel heads west and the other continues southwards. The splashing has grown steadily louder – Maouk's men are gaining on you.

If you wish to head west, turn to **135**.
If you wish to continue south, turn to **164**.

The chest is plain except for a small square of red metal bolted to the top. There is no lock, but, instinctively, you avoid opening the lid with your hands in case it is booby-trapped. Nearby, you notice a wooden bucket and a ladle. Using the ladle, you lever open the chest and push back the lid. The chest itself is not booby-trapped but your caution was well-placed; coiled on a bed of jewel-encrusted maces lies a Yas, a non-poisonous but very large Vassagonian snake. A red forked tongue flicks out of its yellow head as it prepares to defend its valuable bed.

If you wish to attack the Yas, turn to **194**.
If you wish to flick shut the lid and leave the armoury by the north door, turn to **14**.

98

The soft shuffle of stealthy feet warns that you are no longer alone. You whirl around and crouch in readiness for combat; it is this automatic reaction to danger that saves you from a drugged needle fired from a blowpipe. As the tiny missile clips the hood of your cloak, you see the firer reach into his belt pouch for another. Behind him are two warriors armed with sharp, barbed tridents. The three block your passage from the vestibule.

If you wish to attack them before the firer can reload his blowpipe, turn to **168**.

If you do not want to attack them and decide to try to dodge the second blowpipe dart, turn to **118**.

99

As you step into the sunlight, a voice rings out above the noise of the crowd. 'There he is!' It is Maouk. He points at you and a dozen Sharnazim draw their scimitars. 'Surrender, Lone Wolf,' he snarls. 'You cannot escape.'

If you wish to fight, turn to **36**.

If you decide to surrender, turn to **176**.

100

The marble door opens into semi-darkness and the musty smell of old parchment wafts through the air. Row upon row of neatly stacked, leatherbound books stand upon marble shelves, each one of which is beautifully decorated with intricate arabesques in fine gold leaf. Judging by the dates and inscriptions, you deduce that these books form a catalogue of all the treasures in the Grand Palace, many dating back hundreds of years.

Every shelf of the small library is filled with books, every shelf, that is, save one where, on a purple silk cloth, lie a Copper Key and a Prism. If you wish to take either, or both, of these items, mark the Prism as a Backpack Item and the Copper Key as a Special Item (which you carry in your pocket) on your *Action Chart*.

There is no exit from the library other than the marble door by which you entered. After satisfying yourself that nothing useful has been overlooked, you close the door and walk back along the corridor. When you reach the junction, you see a patrol of palace guards ascending the stairs. Without a moment's hesitation, you run towards the east door to avoid being seen.

Turn to **57**.

101

The man screams and keels over, writhing on the floor for a few moments before exhaling his last breath. Meanwhile, his partner has scrambled to his feet, forgetting his weapon in his hurry to escape along the passage. You give chase, pausing only to snatch up the discarded trident; you know you must stop him before he warns other guards. You draw back the trident and throw. It strikes him squarely in the back, pitching him forward as it makes impact. He is dead before he hits the floor.

A search of the dead bodies uncovers the following items:

> 4 Gold Crowns
> 1 Dagger
> 1 Sword
> 1 Potion Alether (Increases COMBAT SKILL by 2 points for the duration of one fight.)

You may also take the Blowpipe and the remaining Sleep Dart. If you decide to keep them, mark them on your *Action Chart* as Backpack Items.

In the robe of the dead blowpipe firer you find a small piece of parchment, on which is written today's date and the number 67. A smile creeps across your face as you realize that this is the number that will open the Bronze Door.

You hold your breath and twist the dial!

Turn to **67**.

102

A thorough search of both bodies uncovers the following items:

> 1 Sword
> 1 Dagger

> 1 Warhammer
> 6 Gold Crowns
> Jailer's Keys (Special Item)

You may take any of the above items. Remember to mark them on your *Action Chart*. The Jailer's Keys should be worn attached to your belt. You remember to lock the cell door before you hurry off along the corridor.

Turn to **150**.

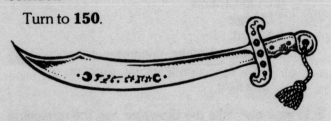

103

You feel your muscles start to relax. The oil soothes the cuts and bruises which cover your body, and restores 2 ENDURANCE points. Make the necessary adjustments to your *Action Chart*.

Turn to **71**.

104

'Take him!' shouts Maouk, 'but take him alive!'

You sprint towards the distant galley. The crew are still unaware of the desperate situation. They have not witnessed the murder of the envoy and are still oblivious to your peril. Before you can shout for help, a horseman cuts across your path, blocking your access to the ship.

If you wish to attack the horseman, turn to **20**.

If you wish to evade combat by diving into the sea, turn to **142**.

If you decide to surrender, turn to **176**.

105

Your attention is drawn to a marble bust standing in an alcove, one of many standing along the south wall. A closer inspection of the bust reveals a hinge at the base of the neck. The head tilts backwards to reveal a tiny lever.

If you wish to pull the lever, turn to **171**.

If you wish to close the head and continue along the corridor, turn to **158**.

106 – *Illustration VI (overleaf)*

You crash on to the rider and pull him from the saddle, but you land badly and lose your grip. The courier is first to stagger to his feet; he unsheathes his sword and attacks before you have a chance to stand up.

Courier: COMBAT SKILL 16   ENDURANCE 23

Deduct 2 from your COMBAT SKILL for the first 3 rounds of combat, as you are still lying on the ground. You cannot evade combat, and must fight the courier to the death.

If you win the combat, turn to **189**.

107

You concentrate all your healing skill on repairing your damaged lung. Gradually, the pain in your chest subsides and a warm glow spreads from the centre of your body, radiating out to your arms and legs. Your

VI.   The courier unsheathes his sword and attacks before you have a chance to stand up

Kai skill heals the wound, but you are still greatly weakened by the loss of blood.

If you wish to search the guard's bodies, turn to **102**.

If you wish to ignore the bodies and escape along the corridor, turn to **150**.

108

Several yards along the new tunnel are more chutes, each covered by an iron grating. Streams of green water pour into the main course, giving off a choking and acrid vapour which attacks your throat and lungs. You wade past the chutes, but you lose 2 ENDURANCE points due to the effects of the corrosive gas. Make the necessary adjustments to your *Action Chart*.

Turn to **112**.

109

You drop to the street below and run across the market-place towards the hall. The building is full of people kneeling in prayer. You notice an avenue leading off to the right, which ends at an archway too narrow for more than one horse to pass. To your left, another alley leads down to the harbour.

If you wish to enter the hall, turn to **32**.

If you wish to turn right and head for the archway, turn to **169**.

If you decide to double back to the harbour, turn to **129**.

110

A gigantic creeping reptile hangs from the ceiling, gripping the stone with its long, curved claws. Its huge oval eyes flicker hungrily as it picks up the scent of live human flesh – your flesh! It is poised to strike and you cannot evade its attack.

Kwaraz: COMBAT SKILL 19   ENDURANCE 30

The giant reptile is very susceptible to psychic power, so if you have the Kai Discipline of Mindblast, add 4 instead of the normal 2 to your basic COMBAT SKILL for the duration of the fight.

If you win the combat, turn to **40**.

111

You are feeling weakened by the heat and by the fatique of combat, but your spirits are high after having beaten such a formidable enemy. You search the armourer's body and discover 3 Gold Crowns and a Copper Key. If you wish to keep the key, put it in your pocket and mark it on your *Action Chart* as a Special Item.

If you wish to leave the forge room by the north door, turn to **167**.
If you wish to leave by the west door, turn to **44**.
If you have the Kai Discipline of Tracking, turn to **74**.

112

You soon reach a section of tunnel where the ceiling is much higher. A stone walkway lines the left wall, with steps at regular intervals. You pull yourself on to the walkway and begin to scrape away the worst of the slime that encrusts your legs.

If you wish to continue along the walkway, turn to **64**.

If you wish to climb a narrow stair in the left wall, turn to **116**.

If you have the Kai Discipline of Animal Kinship, turn to **133**.

113

The passage ends at a tree-lined plaza. You must find somewhere to hide; your fair skin and your Kai cloak and tunic make you stand out in the city crowd.

To your left is a small dwelling with a curious wooden sign hanging above the door, carved in the shape of a fish. To your right is a tavern. The sign above the tavern door seems oddly appropriate:

THE HUNTED LORD

If you decide to enter the dwelling, turn to **157**.

If you decide to enter the tavern, turn to **188**.

If you posses the Kai Discipline of Healing, turn to **53**.

114

You reach a point where the chimney is no longer a vertical shaft, but curves into a horizontal tunnel leading south. Although the heat is oppressive, the steam has cleared. Every nerve and tissue in your body seems agonizingly sensitive and you progress along the narrow shaft with difficulty.

All hope of signing a peace treaty with the new Zakhan has vanished; your only concern now is to escape from this hellish sewer and somehow get back to Sommerlund as quickly as possible.

You notice a square vent cover in the ceiling less than ten feet ahead. It is badly corroded and you have to lie on your back and kick with both feet to force it open. The effort drains your last reserves of stamina, but you are rewarded with success.

By pure chance you have gained access to the one place in Barrakeesh you most need to visit – the public baths.

Turn to **90**.

115

Placing your ear close to the keyhole, you hear faint but horrible sounds. Screams of agony mingled with hysterical laughter and heart-rending sobs. The crack of a whip and the creaking of a rack confirm your suspicions that a torture chamber lies beyond this door. The terrible sounds make you shudder, and you waste no time in hurrying away from the chamber by the north corridor.

Turn to **132**.

116

You climb the stone steps to a small chamber above the tunnel. Here, at least, it is dry, even though the foul sewer gas permeates everything. You follow a narrow passage, first to the west, then to the south as it makes an abrupt left turn. Your heart sinks as you see a dead end loom ahead.

If you wish to search for a hidden exit, turn to **33**.
If you decide to turn around and go back to the walkway, turn to **64**.

117

The twisting alley comes to an end in a small garden square flanked on three sides by tall, domed houses all with first floor balconies. Wrought-iron grilles reinforce every window and door.

You are near the top of a heavy wooden trellis that hangs below a balcony, when Maouk's men burst into the square. Many are armed with heavy bronze crossbows.

'Surrender, Lone Wolf!' shouts Maouk, 'or my men will pin you to the wall!' The situation is hopeless; at such short range, the Sharnazim cannot fail to hit you. Cursing your misfortune, you leap to the ground, landing at the feet of Maouk. 'You are brave, Kai Lord,' he snarls. 'But you will need more than bravery to save you now!'

Turn to **176**.

118

The guard raises the blowpipe to his lips. His cheeks swell and then there is a sharp hiss warning you that another tainted needle now speeds towards your head.

Pick a number from the *Random Number Table*. If you have the Kai Discipline of Hunting, add 2 to the number you have picked. If you have reached the Kai rank of Warmarn or higher, add 1 to the number.

If your total score is now *0–3*, *turn to* **89**.
If your total is now *4–12*, turn to **21**.

119

You catch both guards totally by surprise. Do not deduct any ENDURANCE points you may lose in the first 3 rounds of combat, due to the surprise and ferocity of your attack. You must fight both guards as one enemy.

Palace Gate Guardians:
COMBAT SKILL 16   ENDURANCE 30

If you win the combat, you quickly hide the bodies before passing through the entrance into the palace gardens beyond.

Turn to **137**.

120

The dagger hisses through the air and thuds into your chest. You gasp at the sudden pain, clawing at the hilt of the dagger with trembling hands in your panic to draw out the deadly blade. As you stagger backwards, the guard rushes forward, a smile of triumph spreading across his ugly face. You wrench the blade free and turn it on the guard as he dives towards you. He sees the danger but far too late – the blade has already pierced his heart.

Turn to **22**.

121

From out of the gloom, three Sharnazim warriors suddenly appear. The razor-sharp edges of their swords glint in the darkness; thirsty blades gasping for your blood.

If you wish to attack the warriors, turn to **60**.
If you wish to evade them, you must turn back and swim across the sewer vault. Turn to **84**.

122

The heavy wooden door is reinforced with bands of black iron, held in place by huge bronze studs. You turn the handle, only to find the door is locked.

If you possess the Jailer's Keys, turn to **136**.
If you do not have this Special Item, turn to **26**.

123 – *Illustration VII (overleaf)*

The noise grows louder. Suddenly the door latch rattles and a gruff voice growls out above the din: 'Break it down!'

Shards of wood and twisted iron are scattered throughout the cellar as the sharp blade of a two-handed axe explodes through the door. The hinges

VII.   The officer, a bull-necked warrior with a flat nose, elbows
the others aside and attacks

burst from the wall and in run your pursuers, stumbling on the tangle of shattered timbers.

You spring forward, striking left and right, and bringing two men down before they even see you. The officer, a bull-necked warrior with a flat nose, elbows the others aside and attacks. You strike first, jarring the scimitar from his grasp with a well-aimed blow to his wrist. He bellows like an ox but attacks again, a long-bladed dagger clenched in his uninjured hand.

Sharnazim Underlord:
COMBAT SKILL 18   ENDURANCE 28

You can evade the combat at any stage by escaping through the trapdoor. Turn to **51**.
If you win the combat, turn to **198**.

124

You leap from the window ledge and crash feet first into the guards, bowling them over with the surprise of your attack. You fight with speed and skill, killing three soldiers before they can regain their balance. However, the noise of combat alerts the mess hall and a dozen more of the Zakhan's soldiers join the battle. You are quickly overwhelmed by the sheer weight of numbers, and it is only their respect for your bravery and combat prowess that prevents them killing you on the spot.

You are disarmed and frog-marched to a prison cell, where you are left to await the Zakhan.

Turn to **18**.

125

The horse and its dead rider topple from the quayside and splash into the sea. The crew have drawn up the gangplank, forcing you to leap the gap. You fall short and land on the row of oars bristling from the galley's side.

The wood is wet and slippery and you have to fight to keep your balance. Pick a number from the *Random Number Table*. If you have the Kai Discipline of Hunting, add 2 to the number you have picked.

If your total is now *0–3*, turn to **50**.
If your total is now 4 or more, turn to **191**.

126

Keeping in the shadow cast by the tomb, you advance on the north gate. Only two soldiers stand guard where there would normally be twenty. Suddenly, the gate opens to admit a rider. He hands a scroll to the guards before galloping through the open gate. The guards read the scroll, seemingly unaware that the gate is still open.

If you decide to attempt to bribe the guards, turn to **19**.
If you decide to attack them, turn to **119**.
If you possess the Kai Disciplines of both Camouflage and Hunting, turn to **170**.

127

You walk back along the corridor to the junction in order to get a long run at the door – you know that if you barge the door in exactly the right place, you will tear loose the lock from the wall. Pick a number from the *Random Number Table* and add 10.

> If your total is equal to or less than your COMBAT SKILL, the wall cracks and the lock bursts open. Turn to **159**.
>
> If your total is greater than your COMBAT SKILL, the door remains locked. You sustain a badly bruised shoulder and lose 1 ENDURANCE point. You must head off dejectedly along the other passage towards the stairs. Turn to **93**.

128

You reach a domed sewer-vault where the tunnel widens. A chute descends from the centre of the chamber, ending just a few feet above the oily surface of the water; a mass of food scraps and offal floats beneath the chute, and the stink of rotting meat is overpowering.

You are about to step into the vault when you detect that the tunnel floor drops away. You freeze just in time to prevent yourself from stepping straight into deep water. The tunnel continues beyond the vault, but over twenty feet of putrid sewage lies between you and the other side.

The echo of a distant splash reminds you that the Sharnazim are still following. If you possess a Rope, you can try to catch it upon a long metal bar that protrudes from the side of the chute to pull yourself out of the water and swing across to the opposite tunnel.

If you decide to try to swim across the vault to the tunnel, turn to **84**.
If you would rather turn round and make your way back to the junction, turn to **121**.
If you have a Rope and decide to use it in the manner described above, turn to **29**.

129

From the shadow of a doorway, you peer out across the harbour. The square is alive with Maouk's soldiers. It will be far too dangerous to enter the harbour; you must find somewhere else to hide until it is safer.

Groups of soldiers are searching the houses that border the square, and you are forced to leave the doorway and run back along the alley. As you re-enter the market-place, you run straight into a dozen Sharnazim led by Maouk himself.

If you wish to stand and fight, turn to **36**.
If you wish to surrender, turn to **176**.

130

You snatch the Herb Pad from the dead warrior's face (mark this as a Special Item on your *Action Chart*) and cover your own mouth with this sweet-smelling pouch. The herbs inside neutralize the foul air, making it easier to breathe. Restore 1 ENDURANCE point.

The dead body sinks from view and you hear the sound of more Sharnazim wading along the tunnel. You cannot outdistance them – you must hide.

> If you possess the Kai Discipline of Camouflage, turn to **151**.
> If you do not have this skill, turn to **15**.

131

You sift through the vast number of items that litter the dais, separating the following articles, which may, or may not be of use:

Silver Comb
Hourglass
Dagger
Healing Potion of Laumspur (restores
    4 ENDURANCE points if swallowed after
    combat)
Prism
Enough food for 3 Meals (each Meal counts as
    1 Backpack Item)

Remember to make the necessary changes to your *Action Chart* before leaving the chamber.

Turn to **58**.

132

You move quickly and quietly along the north corridor, and soon arrive at another arched passage that heads off to the west. A fierce glow can be seen in the distance and you hear the hiss of red-hot steel as it is thrust into water and the clang of hammer on anvil— the unmistakable sounds of a blacksmithy.

If you wish to go west, towards the noise, turn to **195**.

If you wish to keep moving north, turn to **30**.

133

You recognize the tracks of a Kwaraz in the slimy mud of the walkway. Kwaraz are giant carnivorous reptiles. The number and varying size of the prints suggest that a whole colony of these loathsome creatures inhabit the tunnel. You decide that it is far too dangerous to continue in this direction, and instead climb a narrow stairway that leads to a chamber above the tunnel. Here at least it is dry, although the foul sewer gas permeates everything. You follow a narrow passage, first to the west and then south, but your heart sinks as you see a dead end looming ahead.

If you wish to search for a hidden exit, turn to **33**.
If you decide to turn round and return to the walkway, turn to **64**.

134

You use your Kai Discipline to force the creature away. The Bloodlug changes direction and jets towards a squid that has taken refuge in a large copper urn. You continue swimming but keep a watchful eye on the Bloodlug as it engulfs and devours the helpless squid.

Turn to **95**.

135 – *Illustration VIII (overleaf)*

The air of the new tunnel is hot and humid, and as you press on, the putrid gas makes you increasingly nauseous. You are forced to stop – the vapour is burning your throat and causing painful stomach cramps. Suddenly a noise makes you forget your discomfort; you turn to see that one of Maouk's men has caught up with you. He looms out of the darkness, his face covered by a pad of herbs.

Sharnazim Warrior:
COMBAT SKILL 17   ENDURANCE 22

Deduct 2 points from your COMBAT SKILL due to the effects of the noxious fumes.

(continued over)

VIII.   One of Maouk's men looms out of the darkness, his face
covered by a pad of herbs

If you lose this combat, turn to **161**.
If you win the combat, turn to **130**.

136

Once you have unlocked the door, you twist the handle and open it a few inches. You see a stair descending to a small chamber where a black-robed soldier is guarding a pair of iron gates. Through the bars you can see rows of weapons and suits of armour stacked in long racks. A sign fixed to the bars says:

GRAND PALACE ARMOURY

If you have the Kai Discipline of Camouflage, turn to **186**.
If you want to attack the guard, turn to **178**.
If you want to close the door and take the other passage, turn to **93**.

137

Suddenly you realize just how hungry you are. You must now eat a Meal or lose 3 ENDURANCE points. You pass unseen through the exotic plants that grow everywhere in abundance. A gravelled path divides a lawn of strange luxuriant purple grass, and leads to a magnificent fountain. A jet of clear blue water catches the sun, reflecting and refracting an eye-dazzling rainbow of colour. You gaze beyond the fountain to where the vaulting towers of the palace soar into the sky, and carefully note the positions of the doors and windows.

There are two entrances to the Grand Palace from the gardens; you can either go through the palace kitchens or through the Vizu-diar – the Zakhan's trophy hall. However, only one of these entrances will lead to the Imperial Apothecary, and to the precious Oede herb stored there.

> If you wish to enter the palace through the kitchens, turn to **66**.
>
> If you wish to enter through the Vizu-diar, turn to **149**.
>
> If you have the Kai Discipline of Tracking or Sixth Sense, turn to **37**.

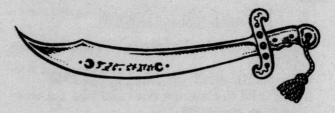

138

The guards pull open the door and you spring into action. Your clenched fist strikes the first man beneath his bearded jaw, lifting him from the floor with the power of the blow. His sword drops from his hand and clatters to the ground close to your feet.

> If you wish to pick up the sword, turn to **4**.
>
> If you wish to ignore the sword and attack the second guard with your bare hands, turn to **91**.

139

You are so irritated by the crawling mask of insects covering your skin, that you fail to see the rusty metal post sticking out of the water ahead. You walk straight into it and lose your footing. Instinctively, you grab at the post, but like everything else it is covered with sewage, as slippery as Kalte ice.

Turn to **94**.

140

The iron gates of the armoury are unlocked. You push open the left gate and wince as the shrill squeak of a dry hinge sends a shiver down your spine.

Inside, at the end of a long aisle, is a workbench, littered with spearheads, sword hilts and all manner of armourer's tools. In the midst of this tangled mess is a large, black, leatherbound book.

If you wish to open the book, turn to **83**.
If you wish to ignore the book and search for your confiscated equipment, turn to **181**.

141

You throw yourself to one side, barely escaping the dart as it whistles past your chest.

'Seize him!' screams Maouk, kicking his soldiers onwards through the wreckage. 'Don't let him get away this time!' You are now lying on the floor less than a couple of feet away from the trapdoor.

If you wish to roll over to the trapdoor and escape, turn to **51**.
If you decide to surrender to Maouk and his warriors, turn to **10**.

142

You hit the water and swim submerged until the pain in your lungs forces you to the surface. Sharnazim are running in every direction, trying to surround the quay and prevent your escape. Gulping another breath, you dive again and swim towards a cluster of small boats less than fifty yards away.

Through the clear blue water, it is easy to see the rubbish that litters the bed of the harbour; mementoes of all the merchant ships that have docked at the quayside. Clinging to one old anchor is a strange jelly-like blob. A mass of short tubes sticks out from all its sides and a long hook-like scoop hangs beneath its rubbery body. Without warning, the blob suddenly jets towards you, propelled by water from its mass of breathing tubes. It is a Bloodlug, and it is hungry for your flesh!

If you have the Kai Discipline of Animal Kinship, turn to **134**.
If you wish to fight the creature, turn to **12**.
If you wish to evade the creature, turn to **95**.

143 – *Illustration IX*

You set light to a tar-coated torch and hurl it down into the sewer-hole. There is a tremendous flash and roar; suddenly, all along the alley, plumes of flaming sewage explode skywards. The alley is transformed into a rush of shocked and screaming people, all scrambling to avoid the deluge of burning filth raining down on their heads. The torch has triggered a chain-reaction in the Baga-darooz; the inflammable sewer gas has ignited – everywhere is panic and confusion.

You run with the crowd through the sewage-stained alleys until you reach a busy market square, unpol-

IX. The alley is transformed into a rush of shocked and
screaming people, all scrambling to avoid the deluge of burning
filth

luted by the blast. Your eye is caught by a sign hanging above the side door of a large hall:

BARRAKEESH PUBLIC BATHS

You push open the door and slip inside.

Turn to **90**.

144

A terrible sense of dread fills your mind. Your Kai skill is warning you that a horrific and inescapable fate awaits you if you stay in this cell. You follow your instincts and attack.

Turn to **174**.

145

You wade into the water, thick with scum, and try not to breathe through your nose. The glutinous mire is clotted with green and black filth, and with your every movement the surface cracks, releasing a vile gas. You cover your mouth with your Kai cloak, but the appalling stench makes you retch and choke. A loud splash behind you warns that Maouk's men are not far away and you quicken your step. At regular intervals, circular chutes disappear into the ceiling. Many are stained bright yellow, white or reddish-brown. This section of the Baga-darooz passes beneath the Linen Quarter of Barrakeesh, where the Guild of Linen-weavers operate their fuller's shops. The chutes dump waste dyes straight into the sewer, making the oily water even more garish in colour.

You spot a ripple in the water ahead. It moves nearer, the wake of a submerged sewer creature. Instinctively, you flatten yourself against the dye-stained wall as you feel the movement of water against your waist, and watch in fear and fascination as the ripple of water disappears into the tunnel. Suddenly, a fearful scream bursts out of the darkness; Maouk has lost one of his men. The terrible cries of the Sharnazim warrior chill your spine, but your instincts tell you to press on while you have the advantage. The channel soon reaches a junction where another tunnel heads off to the west.

If you wish to enter the new tunnel, turn to **108**.
If you wish to continue northwards, turn to **70**.

146

For a few minutes, you watch the man working at his anvil, in case he, too, should decide to leave the chamber. However, he continues to work, apparently unaffected by the scorching heat.

To reach the west door without being seen, you must make your way cautiously across the chamber, dodging from one pillar to the next. Pick a number from the *Random Number Table*. If you have the Kai Discipline of Camouflage or Hunting, deduct 2 from the number you have chosen.

If your total is now less than 2, turn to **44**.
If your total is now 3 or more, turn to **190**.

147

Your Kai sense tells you to beware of the man who helped you. He intends to betray you for a purse of silver.

If you wish to stay in his house, turn to **61**.
If you wish to escape by the window, turn to **109**.

148

As soon as you enter, the panel slides shut and you are plunged into darkness. You advance nervously, your hand held before your face to part the cobwebs that hang in festoons from the low ceiling. You are a few feet away from what appears to be a dead end when you tread on a pressure plate, which activates another panel that slides back to reveal a small chamber.

Turn to **14**.

149

You reach the door to the Vizu-diar without being seen, only to find that it is securely bolted from the inside. You are about to curse your bad luck when you notice a window set into an elaborately carved panel above the door; its iron shutter is open.

In spite of your injured arm, you successfully climb the nail-studded door and drop through the window into the silence of the trophy room. An eerie collection of stuffed heads lines the walls of this private chamber. Most are those of reptilian desert creatures, souvenirs of imperial hunting expeditions into the Dry Main. Among the snake-like trophies, and more gruesome, are human heads! They are ghoulish battle honours, the heads of enemy commanders slain in battle during the countless wars waged by Vassagonia.

You hurry out of the Vizu-diar and into a long marble corridor, where the walls are inlaid with veins of gold and pearls. It leads to a large hall where palace guards and brightly robed courtiers are walking to and fro, but a colonnade of statues provides all the cover you need to reach a distant staircase unseen. Stealthily, you sprint up the staircase to arrive at a junction where passages head off to the east and west. At the end of each is a door with a symbol engraved into the wall above. The symbol above the east door depicts a mortar and pestle; the symbol above the west door, an open book.

If you wish to investigate the east door, turn to **57**.
If you wish to investigate the west door, turn to **100**.

150

The corridor heads north but soon ends at a junction where another passage runs across from east to west. Cautiously, you peer around the corner, but there are no signs of any guards. At the end of the east passage you can see a flight of steps descending out of view; to the west, you see a closed door.

If you wish to go east, towards the stairs, turn to **93**.
If you decide to go west, towards the door, turn to **122**.

151

Your keen eye falls upon a narrow fissure in the tunnel wall. The gap is near to the level of the scum and can barely be seen in the darkness. You squeeze inside, steeling yourself as the foul water rises up to your chin. The Sharnazim pass within inches of your hiding place and you have to fight the urge to vomit as a wave of sewage laps your face. 'He has taken the south tunnel,' echoes an angry voice. 'Quickly – don't waste your time here!'

It seems an eternity before the Sharnazim retrace their steps and disappear back along the tunnel. With a sigh of relief, you emerge from the fissure, but catch your foot in something embedded in the silt of the tunnel floor and lose your balance.

Turn to **94**.

152

You press yourself against the weathered stone, and try to avoid looking down at the courtyards and gardens of the palace, hundreds of feet below. You bite your lip and wait for the guards to pass; but they do not pass. It is nearly sunset and they have come to shut the iron grilles of the palace windows. You hear the creak of dry hinges and the click of bolts – sounds that send a shiver down your spine. You realize that you are now locked out.

To your left, the ledge continues around the outside of a dome; inside this is the mess hall. If you can only inch your way around the tower, you may be able to find an open window on the other side.

Pick a number from the *Random Number Table*. If

you have the Kai Discipline of Hunting, add 2 to the number you have picked. If you have reached the Kai rank of Savant, you may add another 2.

If your total score is now *0–2*, turn to **5**.
If your total score is now *3–8*, turn to **38**.
If your total score is now *9–13*, turn to **87**.

153

Maouk orders his black-clad troops to search the area, threatening them with death if they allow you to escape. You bite your lip and wait for a chance to run.

Creeping from one boat to the next, you reach a narrow flight of stone steps. At the top of the steps, beyond a small paved square, lies a maze of crooked alleyways that disappear into the shadows of the Thieves' Quarter. You are less than twenty feet from safety when a cry echoes across the water! 'There he is.'

You sprint along a deserted passage and climb a stairway into an open courtyard. The sound of hooves clattering on the cobblestones below urges you onwards. There are three possible exits from the courtyard: a high, nail-studded gate to the left; an alley to your right; and a straight, paved pathway that leads to an arch. You must make a quick decision for Maouk's men are close at your heels.

If you wish to enter the gate, turn to **75**.
If you wish to enter the alley, turn to **117**.
If you decide to take the straight pathway through the arch, turn to **169**.
If you possess the Kai Discipline of Tracking, turn to **42**.

154

You part the bead curtain that hangs across the doorway and enter the cool interior. The light is poor and the room gloomy, for the windows are obscured by sheaves of herbs and plants. You are studying a curious row of coloured bottles when a woman appears. She has piercing green eyes and her red hair is raised, bound with rings of jadin. Softly, she speaks to you.

'Welcome, Northlander. I sense you are a warrior – or am I mistaken?' As you hesitate to answer, she shrugs her shoulders and searches through a pile of parchments stacked on top of a wine casket. She blows away the dust before handing you a yellowed sheet. It is a list of merchandise, written in Sommlending:

Potion of Alether (increases COMBAT SKILL by 2 for the duration of 1 combat) – 4 Gold Crowns

Potion of Gallowbrush (induces sleep for 1–2 hours per dose)– 2 Gold Crowns

Potion of Laumspur (restores 4 ENDURANCE points per dose) – 5 Gold Crowns

Vial of Larnuma Oil (restores 2 ENDURANCE points per dose) – 3 Gold Crowns

Tincture of Graveweed (causes sickness and loss of 2 ENDURANCE points per dose) – 1 Gold Crown

Tincture of Calacena (causes terrifying hallucinations for 1–2 hours per dose) – 2 Gold Crowns

You may purchase any of the above; all potions, vials and tinctures are Backpack Items. You then leave the shop and continue along the street..

Turn to **179**.

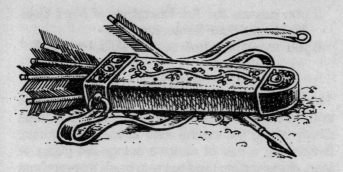

155

From the view, you judge that this window is set high up in the south wall of the Grand Palace. Far below you can see the buildings of the capital, in miniature clusters inside the white city wall. To the south-east lies Lake Inrahim, an immense salt-water plain that is completely dry and cracked. To the north, a road stretches across the causeway to the town of Chula, just visible on the horizon. To the south-west lie the barren, sun-scorched Dahir mountains and the shifting ocean of sand known as the Dry Main.

The bars of the window are badly corroded; it would be easy to dislodge them. However, the drop of several hundred feet to the city below means that there is no hope of escape this way. You climb down from the table and hurry along the corridor.

Turn to **182**.

156

After concentrating on the lock for several minutes, you realize that it is connected to an alarm. If you turn the lock to the wrong number, the alarm will be triggered, alerting the entire palace guard.

If you possess the Kai Disciplines of Mind Over
    Matter and Sixth Sense, turn to **8**.
If you do not have both of these skills, turn to **98**.

157

The house smells strongly of burnt incense. You
enter a narrow hallway lined with chairs and walk
slowly along the central aisle towards a fountain,
flanked by a pair of massive orange-red pillars. A
man, dressed from head to toe in black, appears from
behind the left-hand pillar and walks towards you.

Suddenly, you hear Maouk's men enter the plaza,
and cast an anxious glance towards the open door.
The man sees that you are nervous and silently points
to a cellar door.

If you wish to hide in the cellar, turn to **16**.
If you wish to leave the hallway, return to the plaza
    by turning to **99**.

158

You enter a gallery, which houses a beautiful mosaic.
Thousands of tiny fragments of pearl and gold
shimmer in the light of the evening sun, glancing
rainbows of colour across the high marble walls. A
group of palace courtiers ambles through the gallery
and you are forced to hide behind a huge pillar. You
wait until their footsteps have faded into the distance
before emerging into the light.

All hope of signing a peace treaty has long vanished,
and your only concern now is to escape from the
Grand Palace and, somehow, return home to
Sommerlund as quickly as possible. Hurrying out of

the gallery, you follow the passage westwards and soon reach a junction where the passage turns abruptly to the north.

Turn to **58**.

You batter your way through the door successfully, but having gathered momentum, you cannot stop, and fall headlong down a flight of stairs on the other side.

You land in a heap on the hard marble floor of an antechamber, (you lose 2 ENDURANCE points) barely a few feet away from an armed soldier, who is guarding the doors to the palace armoury. He is startled by your dramatic entrance, but quickly regains his senses and attacks.

Armoury Guard: COMBAT SKILL 16   ENDURANCE 22

Deduct 2 from your COMBAT SKILL for the first 3 rounds of combat, as you are lying on the ground. You cannot evade combat, and must fight the guard to the death.

If you win, turn to **52**.

Your desire to leave this treacherous city is overcome by your fear of losing your arm. You must get the Oede herb, even though it means you will have to enter the very place you are most anxious to avoid – the Grand Palace.

The alley follows a tortuous route through the Mikarum, finally leading you to the 'Horm-tas-Lallaim': the Tomb of the Princesses. Beyond the tomb, the Grand Palace rises like a massive white pantheon.

You suddenly recall a legend told to you by your Kai masters long ago: 'The Nemesis of the Black Zakhan'. The Black Zakhan was a brutal tyrant, the cruellest of an evil lineage that ruled over the desert empire long ago. The barbaric excesses of his reign have never been forgotten in the Lastlands. The Grand Palace was built by his army of slaves, prisoners from countries he had conquered in war. The palace became his obsession; he personally oversaw its entire construction, and punished the workers personally if there was the slightest delay. He butchered his subjects indiscriminately and in the most terrible fashion. His favourite form of execution was for the victim to be sawn in half from head to foot, until the body fell into two pieces. However, it was the mass execution of the slaves who built the Grand Palace, that made him infamous. He slaughtered every slave worker so that his enemies could never learn of the secret treasure chambers he had had constructed. Among the slaves were his only daughters, Kebilla and Sousse, who openly opposed their father's cruelty and tried to prevent the executions. In a blind rage, he ordered that they should be the first to die.

It would have been better for the Zakhan, and for Vassagonia, if he himself had died that day. He lived for another two years, but his mind was unhinged by guilt, and he was tortured by self-loathing and despair. In the Grand Palace, the silence of the night was frequently broken by the Zakhan's moans and cries, as he wandered from room to room looking for his daughters. When he died, he was laid beside them, here, in the Tomb of the Princesses.

From where you stand, you can see two entrances to the Grand Palace; a spike-topped gate in the north wall, and an arch in the west wall, blocked by an iron portcullis. The palace is usually heavily guarded, but there are very few guards today; most are searching for you in the city.

If you wish to approach the north gate, turn to **126**.
If you wish to approach the west arch, turn to **79**.
If you wish to search for some other way of entering the Grand Palace, turn to **49**.

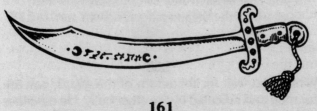

161
You are very lucky that your enemy was only trying to knock you unconscious. Restore half the ENDURANCE points you lost in combat.

Turn to **69**.

162 – *Illustration X*

You pull yourself into the left chimney and pause to catch your breath. The scalding steam hurts your lungs; and every move becomes a tremendous strain, for your hands and face are now swollen and sore. Lose 1 ENDURANCE point before continuing your climb.

You hook your fingers into a jagged crack in the wall of the sweltering chimney and try to draw yourself upwards. Suddenly, a wave of fear engulfs you – something is crawling up your forearm. You have disturbed a nest of loathsome arachnids.

Steamspiders: COMBAT SKILL 10   ENDURANCE 35

These creatures are immune to Mindblast. If you have lost the use of one arm, you cannot fight these biting horrors for you will inevitably slip and fall into the tar-sorkh. Pick a number from the *Random Number Table*. This represents the number of ENDURANCE points that you lose (0 = 10) as you climb past the Steamspiders' nest.

If you are still alive after climbing past the nest, or if you fight the Steamspiders and win, turn to **114**.

163

While you wait for the return of the guard, you are taunted and ridiculed by the other bully. He describes with relish all the horrible tortures that await you, and is greatly disappointed when the other guard returns empty-handed. 'The Zakhan doesn't want our northern friend damaged. He's got something special planned for him this evening,' he snarls.

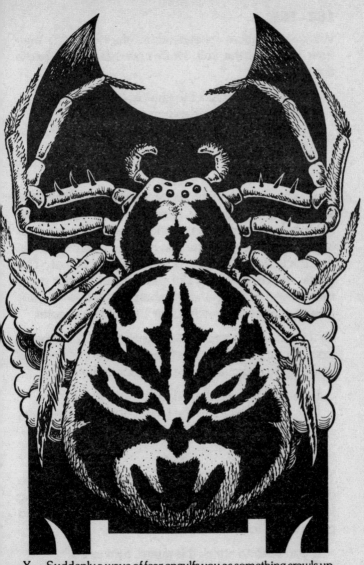

X.   Suddenly a wave of fear engulfs you as something crawls up
your forearm

Wicked grimaces spread across their faces as they turn to leave the cell. Both now have their backs towards you.

If you wish to attack the guards, turn to **174**.
If you wish to remain as you are, turn to **18**.
If you have the Kai Discipline of Sixth Sense, turn to **144**.

164

The water is becoming thicker, and the stench of the sewer gas increasingly more vile and nauseating. Suddenly the air becomes choked with thousands of tiny flies, and every time you gasp for breath you feel the thick fur of pulped bodies in your throat. The black specks build up like paste around your eyes, mouth and nostrils, and the sharp tangy taste in your mouth makes you retch. Lose 1 ENDURANCE point.

As if in answer to your prayers, an iron ladder appears from out of the gloom. It is fixed to the tunnel wall and leads up to a circular stone trapdoor in the ceiling.

If you wish to climb the ladder, turn to **31**.
If you wish to ignore the ladder and press on along the insect-choked tunnel, turn to **139**.

165

The guard clutches at his wounds and drops lifeless to the ground. You see that the other man is recovering from your blow and is clawing at the cell door to try to pull himself to his feet.

If you wish to attack this guard, turn to **78**.
If you wish to overpower him and capture him alive, turn to **199**.

166

You knead your numb arm in an effort to massage some life back into it, but it is useless; the muscles are limp and nerveless. The only consolation is that it is not your weapon arm, but as long as you are suffering from this disease, you cannot use a shield of any sort. Deduct 3 points from your COMBAT SKILL – the lost points may be recovered if ever you should regain the use of your arm.

You turn your attention to your surroundings in an effort to find some way of escape from the nightmarish sewer. The passage ahead winds and curves like a giant snake, and the foul air that drifts towards you is hot and humid. You have shaken off your pursuers, but you now have the problem of your arm to solve.

Turn to **55**.

167

You pass through the door and hurry into the welcoming cool of the room beyond. You notice a large drawbar on this side of the door, and instinctively lock it to delay any would-be pursuers. The room is empty, save for some clothing draped over the back of a wrought-iron chair. Judging by the size and cut of the material, the clothes must belong to the armourer.

You can hear noises echoing from a passage to the east; the voices of hungry guards and the dinstinctive clatter of plates.

You climb a wide stairway and follow a network of passages towards the west. They are lined with alcoves that contain marble busts and beautiful tapestries, each depicting a past Zakhan or a long-forgotten battle.

If you have the Kai Discipline of Sixth Sense, turn to **105**.
If you do not possess this skill, turn to **158**.

168

With a tiger-like bound you are among the startled guards. The blowpipe firer raises his weapon, but a well-aimed kick to the forehead counters his move. He sommersaults backwards, cracking his head against the wall with a sickening thud. A trident flashes towards your ribs; you sidestep and grab the haft with your free hand, pulling the guard off balance. He stumbles forward and falls flat on his face. You turn just in time to face the third guard – his trident is poised to stab you.

Vestibule Guard: COMBAT SKILL 15   ENDURANCE 23

If you win the combat and the fight lasts 3 rounds or less, turn to **101**.
If the fight lasts longer than 3 rounds, turn to **46**.

169

You enter a wide street where vendors compete for space for their stalls beneath the overhanging balconies. The market is crowded with people; they each wear a black sash as a mark of respect to their dead Zakhan, but here, unlike in most of Barrakeesh, business continues as normal.

You pass a stall festooned with black sashes, each costing 2 Gold Crowns. If you wish to buy a sash, pay the vendor and mark it on your *Action Chart* as a Special Item (which you wear over your tunic). You hurry away from the stall and dodge into a narrow passage lined with eating houses and small taverns, where the smell of food is mingled with the odour of stale wine, and the air is alive with chatter and gossip. Your attention is drawn to a notice freshly pasted to a tavern wall. The bold headline reads:

THE ZAKHAN IS DEAD– LONG LIVE THE ZAKHAN

If you wish to stop to read the poster, turn to **88**.

If you wish to continue along the passage, turn to **113**.

170

The combined mastery of these Kai Disciplines enables you to slip past the guards undetected. By the time they resume their correct guard positions, you have safely made your way into the palace gardens.

Turn to **137**.

171

A panel in the alcove slides aside to reveal a secret, dark and very narrow passage. A pair of footprints can clearly be seen in the dust-covered floor, leading into the darkness.

If you wish to enter the secret passage, turn to **148**.
If you decide to avoid the passage, close the secret panel and continue along the corridor, and turn to **158**.

172

'Come in, stranger. Welcome to my humble tavern,' says the plump landlady of the eating house. 'We have wine and food and rooms a-plenty.'

At this moment, you hear Maouk's men enter the plaza and cast an anxious glance towards the open door. The landlady sees that you are nervous; she points to the cellar stairs and says in a hushed voice: 'Do not worry – we share your fear of the new Zakhan. Quickly, you must hide.' There is no time to hesitate. Maouk's warriors are already approaching the tavern.

Turn to **16**.

173

Judging by the direction of the sluggish flow, the right channel appears to head off to the north. The vast tide of sewage and garbage from the Baga-darooz is swept out towards the coast, until it emerges at Chiras, a village north-west of the capital. There it makes life both difficult and unpleasant for the poor local fishermen (especially during the summer months). If you take the north channel, you should eventually reach the coast.

The left channel heads south, running below the very heart of the capital. In the maze of tunnels that feed into the Baga-darooz, you should be able to find at least one exit to the streets above.

Straight ahead, the channel leads off to the west. It is by far the least fetid and contaminated of the three. During the voyage, you remember 'The Stink' telling you about the Grand Madani: a great aqueduct over forty miles long, which channels fresh water from the river Da into the city. As a result, the citizens of Barrakeesh, unlike the inhabitants of other Vassagonian cities, enjoy a lavish supply of pure water. The west channel will lead to that water source.

If you wish to take the north channel, turn to **145**.
If you wish to take the south channel, turn to **96**.
If you wish to take the west channel, turn to **13**.

174

You spring forward and strike the taller of the guards, slamming your clenched fist into the nape of his neck. He groans and sinks to his knees, his sword clattering to the ground close by your feet.

If you wish to pick up the sword, turn to **4**.
If you wish to ignore the sword and attack the second guard with your bare hands, turn to **91**.

175

Before you find a suitable hiding place, three Sharnazim wade into view. 'Leave him to me, you fools!' booms a voice, and the warriors make way for Maouk who appears from the shadows, a dart held high in his hand. He hisses a curse and flings the missile at your chest.

Turn to **25**.

176

You are stripped of your Backpack, your Weapons, your Gold and all of your Special Items. Your hands are tied behind your back and you are pushed head first into the waiting carriage. 'Back to the palace!' commands Maouk as he climbs aboard and slams the door. 'The Zakhan awaits his prize.'

You fight to free the cords that bind you, but Maouk is quick to see the danger. He grabs your arm and forces a dart into your skin. As sleep engulfs your senses, you hear Maouk's wicked laughter fading into silence.

Make the necessary adjustments to your *Action Chart*, and list all the items that you have had confiscated on a separate sheet of paper, for reference in case you should discover them later in your adventure.

Turn to **69**.

177 – *Illustration XI*

As you strike the Kwaraz a killing blow, three Sharnazim wade out of the dark sewer. They have discarded their black robes and they are naked to the

XI. Three Sharnazim wade out of the dark sewer, naked to the waist

waist. Their muscular chests are decorated with a large, blue tattoo of an eagle's claw. As they struggle out of the water, they fix you with a malicious stare and unsheathe razor-sharp scimitars.

If you wish to attack the Sharnazim, turn to **60**.
If you wish to evade them by climbing the narrow stone stairs, turn to **43**.

178

You are half-way down the stairs when the guard realizes what you are doing. He leaps to his feet and unsheathes his sword; you cannot evade him now and you must fight to the death.

Armoury Guard: COMBAT SKILL 16   ENDURANCE 22

If you win the combat, you may search his body, and turn to **52**.
If you would rather ignore the body and enter the armoury, turn to **140**.

179

All manner of strange and exotic plants, oils, potions and medicaments fill the shop windows, and the smell of the herb-filled street is intoxicating. There is a sudden bustle of activity at the end of the street. The crowd disperses, melting into the shops as if into thin air. A man stands before you, his face is streaked with sweat, his turquoise robes torn and heavily stained. It is Maouk– he has survived the Baga-darooz.

'Were it not for the Zakhan, I would kill you here and now,' hisses Maouk, his face a mask of hate. 'But I will not lose my head for a cowardly Sommlending.'

His insult enrages you, but you control your anger. You sense he is not alone; eyes are watching you at every window.

If you wish to attack Maouk, turn to **197**.
If you wish to turn and run back along the street, turn to **92**.

180

As your enemy collapses at your feet, you notice that the other guard has recovered from your punch. He pulls a dagger from his boot and draws back his hand to throw.

If you possess the Kai Discipline of Mindblast, turn to **45**.

If you do not possess this skill, pick a number from the *Random Number Table*. If you have the Kai Discipline of Sixth Sense or Hunting, add 3 to the number you have picked.

If your total is now *0–5*, turn to **120**.
If your total is now *6–12*, turn to **193**.

181

You root through all the drawers and cupboards of the workbench, smashing locks when they refuse to open, only to be disappointed. These drawers and cupboards do not contain your missing equipment.

All hope of signing a peace treaty with the new Zakhan has vanished; your only concern now is to find your equipment, escape from the Grand Palace and, somehow, return home to Sommerlund as quickly as possible. You pull aside a latticed partition and enter a small antechamber. Narrow stone steps lead up to an open door in the north wall, beside which stands a wooden chest.

> If you wish to climb the steps and enter the door, turn to **14**.
>
> If you wish to investigate the wooden chest, turn to **97**.

182

You arrive at a high-vaulted chamber with a large, nail-studded door set into the south wall. A rack standing near to the door holds a Spear and a Broadsword. You may take either or both of these if you wish. To the north, beneath a beautifully decorated horseshoe arch, is another passage that leads out of the chamber.

> If you wish to enter the passage, turn to **132**.
>
> If you wish to listen at the door, turn to **115**.

183

The warrior's head suddenly emerges from the sewer hole. He lashes at your legs tearing a nasty gash in your calf. You lose 2 ENDURANCE points. In anger and pain, you raise your foot and stamp on the man's head with all your strength. He screams and falls back into the sewer, and you hear a loud, resounding splash. You replace the stone lid and drag a heavy barrel across it before making your way through the maze of city streets.

All hope of signing a peace treaty with the new Zakhan has vanished; your only concern now is to escape from Barrakeesh and, somehow, return to Sommerlund as quickly as possible. Eventually, you reach a busy market square. Your eye is caught by a sign hanging above the side entrance to a large building:

BARRAKEESH PUBLIC BATHS

By this time, the smell of your clothes is making you feel quite ill. You have no hesitation in opening the door and slipping inside.

Turn to **90**.

184

As you stare out across the harbour, you notice a large, white-domed warehouse near to the water's edge. A platform on the upper floor overhangs a merchant dhow moored at the quay below. On this platform are several earthenware tuns: huge spice containers destined for the trading emporiums of Ragadorn. You focus your attention on one of these tuns and concentrate all your Kai skill into making it move. Sweat pours down your face from the strain, but you soon hear a distant crash that confirms your success. The tun has fallen and shattered on the deck of the dhow.

Turn to **153**.

185

The footsteps grow louder and then suddenly stop. You hear whispering and Maouk slowly appears from the shadows, his henchmen at his heels. 'Caught like a wolf in the trap,' he sniggers, a dart held high in his sinewy fist. He hisses a curse and flings the missile at your chest.

Turn to **25**.

186

Using your Kai skill to disguise your Sommlending accent, you call out to the guard. 'Quick! We need your help – the Northlander is escaping!'

Immediately, the guard leaps to his feet and charges up the stairs towards the door. You wait until he reaches the top step before you attack – one kick to the knee sends him tumbling backwards into the chamber, where he falls in a heap at the foot of the stairs. You enter the chamber, poised to strike again should the guard recover and attack. However, this time your caution is unnecessary; the guard is dead, his neck was broken in the fall.

If you wish to search his body, turn to **52**.
If you wish to ignore the body and enter the armoury, turn to **140**.

187

You recognize the creature; it is a Kwaraz, a giant, creeping reptile. Kwaraz are native to the Maakenmire swamp, hundreds of miles to the west of Vassagonia, but they thrive in any hot, damp and fetid environment, and it strikes you that the Baga-darooz sewer is an ideal breeding ground for these deadly beasts. The Kwaraz moves along the ceiling, gripping the stone with its long curved claws, its oval eyes opening wider and wider.

Kwaraz are very susceptible to psychic power. By using your Kai Discipline of Animal Kinship, you persuade it that you are not at all appetizing, and it soon loses interest. You watch with a mixture of fear and fascination as the huge reptile disappears along the tunnel. Suddenly, a fearful scream bursts out of the darkness; Maouk has lost one of his men. A shiver runs down your spine, but your instincts tell you to press on while you have the advantage.

Turn to **17**.

188

The tavern is crowded with people who are seated at a long, stone counter decorated with fragments of coloured marble. Large earthenware jars, full of spicy foods, are set into the counter, and serving girls are busy attending to the hungry customers.

If you are wearing a Black Sash, turn to **172**.
If you do not possess a Black Sash, turn to **72**.

189

The courier screams as he falls, but is dead before his head hits the cobblestones. You waste little time dragging his body into the shadows. You don his loose robe and raise the hood, concealing your tunic and your face. In the pocket of the robe you find a scroll: the pass needed to enter the Grand Palace.

The dead courier's horse has bolted and fled, but

your appearance at the gate on foot does not seem to arouse any suspicion. The guards inspect the scroll with bored indifference, and allow you to pass through the gate into the palace gardens beyond.

Turn to **137**.

190 – *Illustration XII*

You have barely taken a dozen steps before you are seen. The giant armourer raises a massive hammer and strides forward, a bloodthirsty snarl escaping from between his clenched teeth. You prepare to defend yourself, but you are momentarily stunned when you see that the hammer is part of his right arm: it is, in fact, an enormous steel fist.

The armourer bellows a war-cry and you react just in time. The hammer tears a chunk of stone from the wall, less than an inch above your scalp.

Hammerfist The Armourer:
COMBAT SKILL 18   ENDURANCE 30

Deduct 2 points from your COMBAT SKILL for the duration of this combat due to the terrible heat of the forge room.

If you win the combat, turn to **111**.

191

You manage to inch your way along the row of oars until you reach the ship's rail, where eager hands catch hold of your cloak and pull you to safety. Maouk's voice booms out across the water. 'Surrender the Kai lord to me. The Zakhan commands it. Your lives and the lives of all your kin will be forfeit if you disobey this order!'

XII. The giant armourer raises a massive hammer and strides forward

The crew stare at each other in sorrow and dismay – they know that Maouk's words are no idle threat. You cannot expect these men to sacrifice their families for you, so you must quickly decide on an alternative plan.

If you decide to surrender to Maouk, turn to **176**.

If you wish to dive overboard and attempt an escape, turn to **142**.

192

The sweltering heat is overwhelming. Three times you nearly slip and fall and are saved only by your quick wits and natural survival instincts from a gruesome end in the tar-sorkh. You manage to climb twenty feet of the chimney, but the price is high. Your fingers and knees are skinned and bleeding, and your legs ache with fatigue. Lose 2 ENDURANCE points.

Turn to **114**.

193

You jump to one side as the dagger whistles towards you, skimming barely an inch from your throat. The guard stares in open-mouthed disbelief. He is now unarmed.

If you wish to attack the guard, turn to **78**.

If you wish to overpower him and capture him alive, turn to **199**.

194

The Yas is a constrictor: it kills its prey by crushing them to death with the coils of its powerful body. Its sleepy eyes have now opened and the red-rimmed slit pupils fix you with a mesmerizing stare. You suddenly realize that the Yas is trying to hypnotize you. Unless you have the Kai Discipline of Mind-shield, deduct 3 points from your COMBAT SKILL for the duration of this combat.

Yas: COMBAT SKILL 14   ENDURANCE 28

If you win the combat, turn to **35**.

195

A forge has been constructed in the centre of a massive circular chamber, its funnel-like chimney stretching up into the roof. The heat had become unbearable long ago, but now you feel as if you have walked straight into a raging furnace.

Two men, naked except for small loin-cloths, work the bellows that feed the forge. Sweat pours from their bodies and they frequently stop to gulp ladlefuls of water from a trough set in the stone floor. An armourer hammers a strip of red-hot iron at an anvil close to the flames. He is massive; his huge, muscled shoulders and powerful chest as wide as the other two men put together.

The bellows men stop work and leave the chamber; one by the door in the north wall, the other by the door in the west wall. The big man continues to hammer at the anvil.

If you wish to follow the man who left by the north door, turn to **11**.

If you wish to follow the man who left by the west door, turn to **146**.

If you wish to attack the armourer working at the anvil, turn to **190**.

If you wish to leave the chamber and retrace your steps along the corridor to take the other passage, turn to **30**.

196

You notice that a large table dominates the room; it is set with wine and meat, and freshly-baked loaves of bread.

If you wish to eat some of this mouth-watering food, turn to **61**.

If you wish to leave the room by the window, turn to **109**.

197

Maouk pulls his hand from his robe, a dart held tightly in his sinewy fist. He hisses a curse and flings the missile at your chest. You gasp with shock as the missile strikes home – you are too close to avoid being hit.

Turn to **25**.

198

As the officer's body slumps lifelessly across the shattered cellar door, the Sharnazim back away and step aside. Maouk himself appears in the doorway, a dart held high in his hand. 'I have you now!' he hisses, and flings the missile at your chest.

Pick a number from the *Random Number Table*. If you have the Kai Discipline of Hunting, add 3 to the number you have picked.

If your total is now *0–6*, turn to **25**.
If your total is now *7–9*, turn to **141**.

199

You grasp the frightened guard in a secure head-lock and threaten to break his neck if he does not answer your questions. He immediately promises to tell you everything he knows. He says that the new Zakhan fears that you are an assassin, sent by his enemies in the west. He claims to hate the new Zakhan himself. He is only a simple jailer, he says, and knows nothing more.

If you have the Kai Discipline of Sixth Sense, turn to **39**.
If you do not possess this skill, turn to **9**.

200

Upon a raised platform, carpeted with scarlet fur, sits the Vassagonian Emperor, Zakhan Kimah. He is robed in gold, but devoid of all ornamentation. In his hand is an orb of black metal, and in his eye an ice-cold cruelty that chills your spine. The Zakhan is a man of awesome countenance, but he pales in the shadow of his companion.

Before him stands the cause of your terror. A helm as black as death itself hides the face, but the stench of decay and a hideous sepulchral voice betray the identity.

'Give me Lone Wolf!'

It is the fell voice of a mortal enemy – a Darklord of Helgedad. As the Zakhan rises to his feet, you notice a flicker of doubt, or perhaps of fear, dim his cruel gaze, but he is quick to mask it. 'He will be brought to you at sunset in exchange for the Orb of Death. It is agreed.'

'You have the Orb,' echoes the chilling voice. 'Give me Lone Wolf!'

The Zakhan hides his fear well, but time is not on his side. The game of bluff he is playing is deadly. However, the fact that he has not been discovered is evidence of his powerful will, for you sense the Darklord is persistently clawing and probing at his mind.

'You will get your Northlander, Lord Haakon,' says the Zakhan, his voice curt with anger, 'when you tell me why your servants defile the Tomb of the Majhan. You claim to have no need for gold and jewels – why then do you plunder the graves of our ancestors?'

A deathly quiet fills the hall; only the unnatural hiss of the Darklord's breath disturbs the silence. 'This land, this insignificant speck of sand, harbours two small thorns that prick our skin. We seek to remove them both – forever. The fledgling Kai, Lone Wolf, is the thorn that denies us Sommerlund. The Tomb of the Majhan hides the other thorn that threatens us – the accursed *Book of the Magnakai*.

Your heart pounds as the words echo in your head. The *Book of the Magnakai*! Suddenly, the reason why you have been enticed into a deadly trap becomes clear, and the sinister truth is revealed.

The *Book of the Magnakai* is one of the oldest legends of Sommerlund. With the wisdom of the Magnakai, Sun Eagle, the first Kai Grand Master, instilled the disciplines into the warriors of the House of Ulnar, the bloodline of your king, that were to save your land from devastation at the hands of the Darklords. The *Book of the Magnakai* was lost hundreds of years ago, but its wisdom was kept alive, handed down through generations of Sommlending warriors so that they could share the strength to resist their eternal enemies, the Darklords of Helgedad.

If the Darklords discover and destroy the *Book of the Magnakai*, the secrets will be lost forever, and when you die, the Kai will become extinct. However, if you discover the *Book of the Magnakai* first and deny the Darklords their prize, all the wisdom of the Magnakai will be revealed to you. Through its wisdom you will become strong, strong enough to reach the ultimate achievement for a Sommlending warrior – to become a Kai Grand Master.

However, the peril and the glory of the quest that lies ahead is distracting you from more immediate danger. To discover this danger and to begin the quest for the *Book of the Magnakai*, turn to Part Two of *Shadow on the Sand*.

Begin your adventure at **201**.

PART TWO

201

Suddenly, you catch sight of two warriors creeping towards you from a passage to your right. They are clad in jet-black armour and scarlet robes, and their hideous death-masks identify them as Drakkar warriors. They are men, but they are evil men, as evil as the Darklords whom they serve.

One of them holds a razor-fanged Akataz, a creeping leathery war-dog, straining on a chain leash. The Drakkar hisses and the Akataz springs towards your throat.

If you wish to fight this creature, turn to **273**.
If you wish to try to evade the attack and escape, turn to **285**.

202

You pass under an arch where two brass-gilded conical towers gleam like gold, and enter a market-place crowded with squabbling merchants. Exotic carpets, brightly coloured material and all manner of foods are being bought, sold and haggled over. The north side of the market-place is devoted to the auction of douggas. These sleek but noisy desert beasts are being paraded, for the benefit of the bid-ders, around a paddock adjoining their stables. Just past the stables, a street vanishes into the Carpet-weavers' Quarter of Ikaresh.

If you wish to investigate the stables, turn to **309**.

If you wish to ask one of the merchants if they know where Tipasa lives, turn to **248**.

If you wish to leave the market-place, continue along the adjoining street, and turn to **386**.

203

There is a sickening and acidic smell as a great gout of green blood gushes from the Vordak's red robe. The creature screams and topples from view, its mangled corpse spiralling downwards.

Sheathing your weapon, you grab the reins and fight to regain control of your injured mount. You have slain the Vordak but the battle is not yet won. The Itikar is losing a lot of blood, and could lapse into unconsciousness at any moment to drop you like a stone on to hard Lake Imrahim. Suddenly you see something in the distance – something that renews your faith in miracles.

Turn to **221**.

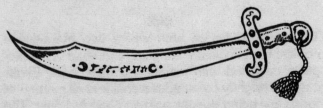

204

You sense that the stone radiates pure evil. If you can only turn the stone's power against the Darklord, it will drain his strength, and make him fade from this dimension. Although the stone cannot kill Haakon, it can at least banish him to a place where he can no longer harm you.

> If you wish to try to grab the stone and turn it on your enemy, turn to **268**.
> If you wish to ignore the stone and attack the Darklord with your own weapon, turn to **390**.

205

All you can hear above the wind that screams past your face are the gleeful howls of the Drakkarim. They are watching you fall to certain doom.

Pick a number from the *Random Number Table*.

> If the number you have picked is 0–4, turn to **234**.
> If the number you have picked is 5–9, turn to **293**.

206

There is no reply to your first knock. You are about to knock again when the door opens a few inches and the red-rimmed eyes of an old woman stare out from the darkness. 'Banedon!' she exclaims, her voice hoarse and shaky. 'Thank the gods it is you.'

She ushers you both inside and locks the door. The house is sparsely furnished and what little there is either damaged or broken. 'They have taken him, Banedon, they have taken my husband – the men with the faces of the dead. Ten days ago. They came like shadows in the night.'

She breaks down, her frail body wracked by sobs. Banedon comforts her as best he can, but you sense he shares her bitter loss. The Drakkarim have taken Tipasa, of that there is little doubt. By now they will have made him tell everything he knows about the Tomb of the Majhan.

'We will find him, I promise,' says Banedon, wiping the tears from the old woman's face, 'but you must try to help us if you can. Tipasa always kept a diary of his travels – do you have it still?'

A flicker of hope shines in the old woman's eyes. 'Yes, it is here. He told me to hide it when the evil men came for him.'

She kneels at an empty fireplace and prises a loose brick from the chimney; a leatherbound book drops from its hiding place into her hand. She gives it to Banedon who studies the yellowed pages, his face lined in thought. You notice that the book is full of cryptic symbols, numbers and pictograms.

'They are drawn by the night stars,' says Banedon, tracing his finger along the astronomical drawings. 'They hold the secret, I know, but without my star charts we cannot hope to find the tomb. We must return to the *Skyrider* at first light. There I shall be able to make some sense of this book.'

Turn to **331**.

207

You discover little of interest: 8 Gold Crowns, and a Brass Whistle on a chain around the guard's neck. You may take these if you wish, but remember to mark them on your *Action Chart*. Suddenly, a noise alerts you to unwelcome company; Drakkarim are rushing along the tiled pathway that leads to the pens.

Without a moment's hesitation, you turn and run inside the Itikar's enclosure.

Turn to **224**.

208

'By the Gods!' cries Banedon. 'A vaxeler!'

The old man's face is a mask of green putrescent sores. The pupils of his eyes are yellow and his ragged grey lips hang in tatters. Banedon grabs your arm and pulls you away from the wretched man.

'He has vaxelus, Lone Wolf, a terrible disease that rots the skin. It is highly contagious – our lives are in peril.

If you possess some Oede herb, you may give it to the poor vaxeler by turning to **321**.

If you do not have any Oede, or if you do not wish to give it to the man, you can flee the cave with Banedon, by turning to **270**.

209

You reach the landing in time to see three Drakkarim warriors enter the tower. Maniacal laughter echoes from their ghoulish death-mask faces, as they form a line and creep towards you.

More of their evil kind are flooding on to the bridge, some carrying crossbows. You decide it would be suicide to attack the Drakkarim, and sprint quickly up the stairs to escape from them.

Turn to **322**.

210

You dive aside, your Kai skill saving you from the axe that is spinning towards the platform. Suddenly, a deafening bang rings out and the Drakkar is flung backwards, his breastplate torn open by dwarf shot. He gives a long, agonizing death-cry as he disappears from sight, tumbling into the darkness that surrounds the speeding sky-ship.

As if in answer to the shot, a menacing roll of thunder rumbles across the darkening plain from Barrakeesh. It is as if the city itself were cursing your escape.

Banedon appears at your side, his face lined with concern. As he offers a shaky hand to help you to your feet, you notice that the makeshift bandage which binds his wound is soaked with blood. He is pale and weak and close to collapse.

If you have the Kai Discipline of Healing, turn to **377**.
If you do not possess this skill, turn to **339**.

211

Despite your misgivings, the lime-green wine tastes delicious. A warm glow radiates slowly from your stomach, filling you with a comfortable sense of well-being. Restore 2 ENDURANCE points. The man looks delighted by your reaction to his wine, and offers to sell you a bottle for 5 Gold Crowns. If you wish to buy a Bottle of Kourshah, pay the man 5 Gold Crowns and make the necessary adjustments to your *Action Chart*. (There is enough Kourshah in the bottle to restore a further 4 ENDURANCE points.)

If you wish to question him about Tipasa the Wanderer, turn to **318**.

If you wish to leave his home and continue on your way to Ikaresh, turn to **272**.

212

Fleeting shadows move through the densely packed trees: the Drakkarim are trying to surround you. Suddenly, a red shape bursts from the foliage and a mace glances across your forehead. You roll with the blow, tumbling over as though stunned by its force. The Vordak shrieks with malicious laughter and leaps upon you, its black mace raised to crush your skull.

If you possess the Sommerswerd, turn to **349**.

If you do not possess this Special Item, turn to **355**.

213

The Drakkar falls to his knees and makes a horrible rasping noise as he tries in vain to prise open his shattered death-mask. Your blows have staved in his helm, and the buckled metal has fractured his skull. You lash out with your foot and kick him from the outrigger, sending him spiralling down to Lake Inrahim to join the dwarf he murdered. But the dwarf is neither dead nor hundreds of feet below. He hangs by his foot, unconscious, snagged in the netting below the outrigger boards. You grab the dwarf's leg and haul him to safety before continuing the fight.

The platform looks empty – no heads are showing above its armoured parapet, but you sense something is wrong. Instinctively, you leap from the outrigger on to the main hull, your weapon poised to strike.

Turn to **361**.

214

You focus your skill on a nearby spade, willing the spade handle to rattle against the wheelbarrow in which it rests. It only takes a few seconds for the vigilant Drakkar sentry to leave his post and investigate the noise. By the time he returns, you are inside the Tomb of the Majhan.

Turn to **395**.

215

At the bottom of the stairs, a wooden door braced with iron blocks the entrance to the scented garden. Frantically you twist the handle, but it does not open – the door is locked. Then a couple of palace guards appear on the bridge above; they see you and unsling their heavy crossbows.

If you possess a Copper Key, turn to **246**.

If you do not possess this item, you can try to climb over the door by turning to **301**.

Alternatively, you can run back up the stairs and attempt to attack the guards before they load and fire their crossbows by turning to **375**.

216 – *Illustration XIII (overleaf)*

You soon enter a public square where a throng of men have gathered at the ruins of a fountain. They are listening to the frenzied speech of a man dressed in red from head to toe; each man in the crowd is wearing a strip of the same coloured cloth, which covers the lower half of his face.

'They're Adu-kaw – "the veiled ones",' says Banedon nervously. 'It sounds as if they're declaring a blood feud on their old enemies, the men of Tefa.'

You follow Banedon to the shelter of a toa tree, where you will be less conspicuous. The speaker is denouncing the Tefarim for imposing a heavy tax for safe passage through their town, and for use of the highway to Kara Kala. His ranting begins to stir the crowd to fever pitch.

Suddenly he points to where you stand and shrieks, 'Tefarim spies!'

> If you want to try to reason with the crowd of screaming fanatics that are now running towards you with their swords drawn, turn to **284**.
>
> If you wish to follow Banedon's example and run for your life, turn to **340**.

217

The Itikar fixes you with a cold, black stare, but you sense that it is no longer hostile. As you settle on its wide saddle, you catch sight of the Drakkarim streaming across the gangplank. Leaning forward, you unhook the anchor rope from the saddle ring, and grab the thick leather reins.

Turn to **343**.

XIII.   His ranting begins to stir the crowd to fever pitch

218

The dwarves continue their meal, pausing only to light large hooded pipes. Through the bluish hue of the pipe smoke that clouds the low cabin roof, you notice that they are casting nervous glances at you, as if you might explode at any moment.

After five minutes have passed, Nolrim raises his tankard and proclaims a toast: 'To Lone Wolf – a man among dwarves!'

The dwarves guffaw at Nolrim's wry toast and raise their tankards in a salute to your courage and fortitude. The Bor-brew has loosened their tongues and they are eager to tell you of their past exploits.

Turn to **291**.

219

You act purely by instinct. You dive to the floor and roll over; the blue flame screams past your head and explodes into the chamber wall, blasting a hole several feet deep in the steel-hard rock. You spring to your feet and dodge behind a massive pillar as the hideous laugh of Darklord Haakon echoes around the dust-choked chamber. As it rises in pitch, your mind is filled with agonizing pain.

If you have the Kai Discipline of Mindshield, turn to **253**.

If you do not possess this Kai Discipline, turn to **369**.

220

Your Kai sense of Tracking reveals that the winding path leads into the Zakhan's arboretum: his cathedral of trees. The stairs to the portal lead to a private chamber in the upper palace, but you still cannot tell what the chamber contains.

If you wish to follow the path, turn to **391**.

If you decide to climb the stairs to the portal, turn to **352**.

221

Emerging from a bank of cloud on the skyline is a flying ship. It is a small craft, no bigger than an Unoram river barge, with two triangular sails swept back either side of its curving prow. In the fading twilight you can make out a long pennant that flutters from its mast. A faint humming reaches your ears. Your first reaction is disbelief; what you are seeing must be a trick of the light or some fiendish illusion created by the Darklords. However, as the ship floats nearer, your senses tell you that it is indeed quite real.

If you possess a Crystal Star Pendant, turn to **336**.

If you do not have this Special Item, turn to **275**.

222

You must act quickly if you are to avoid detection, for the creature in red is a Vordak: one of the powerful undead who serve the Darklords.

Pick a number from the *Random Number Table*.

If you number you have picked is *0–2*, turn to **378**.

If the number is *3–9*, turn to **262**.

223 – *Illustration XIV*

Suddenly, the pain subsides – but the onslaught has only just begun. A mist as black as the grave is seeping

XIV. A deadly flood of horror hurtles from his hand

from Haakon's mouth. It creeps along his out-stretched arm and settles like a cloud in the palm of his upturned hand. Whirling shadow-shapes draw into focus; wings and tentacles sprout and take form. A curse in the dark tongue shakes the whole chamber as a deadly flood of horror hurtles from his hand.

Crypt Spawn: COMBAT SKILL 24   ENDURANCE 40

If you win the combat, turn to **353**.

224

The great black bird beats its massive wings, cawing hoarsely through the domed pen. Two black eyes, fierce and cold, fix you with a deadly stare as you edge nearer to its perch.

Grabbing the saddle pommel, you haul yourself up, but suddenly there is a flash of razor sharp talons. Instinctively, you shield your face as a glint of orange sunlight is caught on the Itikar's curved beak, for it slashes the air barely inches above your head.

If you have the Kai Discipline of Animal Kinship, turn to **308**.

If you possess an Onyx Medallion, turn to **319**.

If you possess neither the Kai Discipline nor the Special Item, pick a number from the *Random Number Table*. If you have reached the Kai Rank of Aspirant or higher, add 2 to the number you have picked.

If your total is now *8–11*, turn to **287**.
If your total is *4–7*, turn to **240**.
If your total is *1–3*, turn to **370**.
If your total is *0*, turn to **257**.

225

The man is short of stature but broad-shouldered and strongly built, physical characteristics common among the tough mountain-dwellers of Vassagonia. He pulls the cork from a bottle of lime-green wine and pours three large measures into earthenware cups.

'Kourshah!' he exclaims, and downs the wine in one swift gulp.

If you wish to follow his example and drink the strange wine, turn to **211**.

If you do not want to drink the wine, ask him where Tipasa can be found, and turn to **318**.

226

You are the first to recover from the surprise of the sudden encounter.

If you wish to attack the guards, turn to **334**. (Ignore any wounds you may sustain in the first 2 rounds of combat.)

If you do not wish to fight them, you can evade before they have a chance to strike at you, by running back up the stairs. Turn to **209**.

227

As you near the entrance to a shadowy alley, you hear a woman's voice begging in the darkness: 'Alms for a poor widow, young sirs?' A decrepit old woman hobbles into the light, her features harsh, her face haggard and drawn. She repeats her plaintive cry: 'Will you spare a coin for a poor window's needs?'

If you wish to stop to question her, turn to **265**.

If you wish to ignore her and continue on your way, turn to **388**.

228

Eager to put distance between yourself and your merciless enemy, you race headlong through a tangle of trees and roots until you stumble upon a small domed hut of latticed wood, half hidden by a curtain of vines. Peering through the dense foliage, you see that the vines reach up to a wrought-iron walkway, which ends at an open stone door.

If you wish to climb up a vine to the walkway and escape through the open stone door, turn to **352**.

If you wish to search for an exit from the arboretum at ground level, turn to **332**.

229

As the craft emerges into the sunlight, a terrible noise fills the air – the screeching cacophony of Kraan-riders, swooping down from the table of rock. They have been waiting patiently for the skyrider to appear before launching their ambush, for they have been certain of your hiding place since before the dawn. The Black Crystal Cube enabled them to track your escape route through the Dahir mountains, its signal to them as clear as a burning beacon in the night.

You sense it is the Cube that has betrayed your escape and snatch it from your pocket, but before you can hurl the accursed object away, it explodes in your hand.

Pick a number from the *Random Number Table*. If you have the Kai Discipline of Sixth Sense, add 3 to the number you have picked.

If your total is now *0–6*, turn to **385**.
If your total is now *7–12*, turn to **251**.

230

There is another searing blast, which hits the base of the huge pillar behind which you have taken refuge; it severs the stone in an instant. Your body is torn to pieces as the pillar explodes into a million fragments – the little of you that remains is buried beneath tons of falling sand and stone.

Your life and the hopes of Sommerlund end here.

231

The Drakkarim rush into the guard room, bellowing like Kalte mammoths and hacking madly at the air with their cruel, black swords. The leader advances on you, a mane of jet-black hair streaming from the open back of his helm, his sword held low for a thrust that will disembowel you. You sidestep and drive your weapon into his armoured chest. The black metal buckles, crushing his ribs, killing him instantly, but before he has fallen to the ground, two more Drakkarim are upon you. You cannot evade combat and must fight them to the death.

Drakkarim: COMBAT SKILL 18   ENDURANCE 34

If you win the combat, turn to **290**.

232

You try to sidestep as the lethal blade hurtles towards you, but in the darkness you cannot be sure of the direction of its flight. You are hit in the chest, the blow smashing the air from your lungs. Lights flash before your eyes and an explosion rings in your ears. You fall to your knees and a sensation of numbness spreads through your chest. Through a haze of swirling mist, you see the Drakkar flung backwards, his breastplate torn open by dwarf shot. Banedon appears; his face is ashen grey. His lips move but you cannot hear what he is saying. Images of Sommerlund swim in your mind and then slowly fade as oblivion engulfs you.

Your life and the last hope of Sommerlund end here.

233

Holding the Prism in the centre of the beam, you divert the light towards the hole in the floor. You hear the sound of stone grating on stone as the door slowly opens to reveal a large chamber. It is dimly lit but in the dust that covers the marble floor you can see footprints too numerous to count. As you enter, you suddenly catch sight of a rough stone throne, facing the wall on the far side of the chamber. Behind you the door slides shut with unnerving speed.

Turn to **289**.

234

In a complete daze you tumble and spin, totally unaware of whether you are falling head or feet first. The warm wind tears at your face, forcing your eyelids and mouth open. You can barely breathe. You scream with terror until you hit the upper branches of a toa tree; in the next instant you hit water. You rapidly surface again, and instinctively begin to pump your legs.

You have no idea in which direction you are swimming, but in three strokes you find yourself at the side of this deep, sculptured pool of clear water. Still shaking from the shock of impact, you claw your way out on to a mossy bank. Miraculously, you have escaped injury, but your ordeal is far from over. The Drakkarim and the palace guards watched you fall and at this very moment are racing down from the tower and the bridge to the palace gardens.

Ahead of you, beyond a tree-lined colonnade, a flight of steps ascends to a small portal in the wall of the upper palace. To your right, a leafy tunnel winds away into the trees and shrubs.

If you wish to climb the stairs to the small portal, turn to **352**.

If you wish to following the winding path, turn to **391**.

If you have the Kai Discipline of Tracking, turn to **220**.

235

Rows of stalactites hang from the roof of the cave, like the fangs of some incredible monster, and the bubbling of a distant geyser echoes eerily through the unknown depths.

You begin to explore, and eventually reach a place where a natural bridge of rock arches over a steaming course of water, red with ore. Huddled beneath the bridge is a pathetic figure, its body bent and emaciated. A tattered blanket covers his face and in his withered hands he clutches a crude fishing rod. A small catch of lavacrabs lie on the bank, their claws twitching as they slowly die. As you move nearer, the figure raises his face to stare at you. It is a man, but the sight of his face shocks you to the core.

If you have the Kai Discipline of Healing, turn to **344**.

If you do not possess this Kai Discipline, turn to **208**.

236

Your speed and stealth carry you across the gangplank undetected. When you strike, the guard is still on his knees, picking up his scattered gold. Your attack is silent and deadly.

If you wish to search the guard's body, turn to **207**.

If you decide to ignore the body, hurry into the Itikar's pen, and turn to **224**.

237

The Jala tastes as good as it smells, and after your dusty trek through the hills, is a welcome relief to your parched throat. Restore 1 ENDURANCE point.

'Do you know where we may be able to find a man called Tipasa the Wanderer?' asks Banedon, successfully hiding his Northland accent with his expert mastery of the Ikareshi dialect.

'I'm sorry, friend, but I have never heard of this man,' replies one of the men.

'You would be wise,' interrupts the other, 'to ask the widow Soushilla. There is little in Ikaresh that she does not know.'

'Where can she be found?' you ask.

'At her tavern, of course,' they reply, simultaneously. 'Cross Eagle Square and you'll find it on the way to the Dougga Market.'

You thank the Ikareshi and leave the eating house. Retracing your steps to the square, you set off towards the Dougga Market in search of Soushilla the Widow.

Turn to **376**.

238

You escape from the combat and sprint along the opposite passage, but the enemy gives chase, and the crunch of iron-shod boots echoes in your ears.

You race down a stairway, through an arch of silver and along a balcony overlooking the lower palace.

You glimpse the silhouette of Darklord Haakon in the hall below, his spiked fist raised. A Drakkar appears from nowhere and leaps at you, his sword raised high above his skull-like helm. There is a deafening crack and a bolt of blue lightning streaks from a stone in the Darklord's hand, and hurtles towards you. The Drakkar lunges and wounds your forearm (you lose 1 ENDURANCE point), but he is now standing in the path of the bolt. In a flash of light, the Drakkar is gone; only cinders and the rotten odour of scorched flesh remain.

At the end of the balcony you see another arch and a staircase.

> If you wish to escape through the arch, turn to **381**.
> If you wish to escape by the stairs, turn to **317**.

239

If you are to get inside the tomb, you must either distract or silence the Drakkar sentry.

> If you possess a Tincture of Graveweed, turn to **260**.

If you do not possess this item, you will have to creep

up and overpower him as quickly and silently as you can. Pick a number from the *Random Number Table.* If you possess the Kai Disciplines of Hunting, Tracking and Camouflage, add 2 to the number you have picked. If you have reached the Kai rank of Guardian, add 3 to the number.

If your total is now *0–4*, turn to **324**.
If it is 5 or more, turn to **303**.

240

Itikar are wild and malicious creatures. It can take several years for a rider to tame and train one but, once tamed, the giant black birds are fiercely loyal. As you approach, the Itikar senses that you are not his master and furiously attacks you with its deadly beak and talons.

Itikar: COMBAT SKILL 17   ENDURANCE 30

Fight the combat as normal, but double all ENDURANCE points lost by the giant bird. When its score falls to zero, you will have subdued it enough to be able to climb into the saddle and take control. All the ENDURANCE points you lose in the combat count as wounds and must be deducted from your current ENDURANCE points total.

If you successfully reduce the Itikar's ENDURANCE points to 0, turn to **217**.

241

Once outside the cave, you and Banedon waste no time in pressing on towards Ikaresh. As you near the outskirts of the town, you pass a small, round hut where a goat is eating from a manger near the door. A man appears in the darkened doorway and bids you welcome; he touches his forehead in a salute of friendship and invites you to enter his humble home.

If you wish to accept his invitation, turn to **225**.

If you decide to decline his offer and continue on your way towards Ikaresh, turn to **272**.

If you have the Kai Discipline of Sixth Sense, turn to **365**.

242

You recognize the creature dressed in red: it is a Vordak, a servant of the Darklords, one of the powerful undead. Vordaks possess great psychic power, and you feel it scanning for you with its Mindforce. You know that if you are to avoid these evil troops, you will not only have to hide, but also shield your mind.

Pick a number from the *Random Number Table*. If you have the Kai Discipline of Camouflage, add 2 to the number you have picked. If you have the Kai Discipline of Mindshield, add 3.

If your total score is now *0–6*, turn to **262**.

If it is 7 or over, turn to **378**.

243

Your deadly stroke hurls the Drakkar over the armoured parapet. He tumbles from view and plummets into the valley thousands of feet below.

Turn to **306**.

244

You can clearly see the main highway that links Chula to the capital. It crosses the desolate salt plain of Lake Inrahim by means of a causeway thirty feet high, and is a useful landmark by which you can steer. Little stone houses with beaten earth roofs are grouped in small clusters along the highway, their numbers increasing as you draw nearer to the town.

You are five miles from Chula, when you notice a dark cloud hovering several hundred feet above one of the small villages. It is a cloud of Kraan; they are moving to intercept you.

Suddenly the Itikar squeals in pain and a splash of feathers billows out from its wing. A Kraan has closed in from behind; it is less than a hundred yards distant. The Drakkar rider holsters an empty bronze cross-bow and draws his black sword. His bolt has passed through the wing of your mount, and he prepares to strike as the Itikar loses height and speed.

Drakkar Kraan-rider:
COMBAT SKILL 20   ENDURANCE 28

The Kraan and its rider are swooping on you from behind. You will only be able to fight for one round of combat before they are carried past by the momentum of their attack.

> If you lose more ENDURANCE points than the enemy
> in this one round of combat, turn to **347**.
>
> If the enemy loses more ENDURANCE points than
> you, turn to **327**.
>
> If you both lose exactly the same number of
> ENDURANCE points, turn to **271**.

245

You remove your Blue Stone Triangle from around
your neck and press it into the indentation in the wall.
It is a perfect fit. You hear the sound of stone grating
on stone, and the door slowly opens to reveal a
chamber. It is dimly lit, but you see that the thick dust
on its marble floor is covered with innumerable footprints. As you enter, you catch sight of a rough stone
throne, facing the wall on the far side of the chamber.

Behind you the stone door slides shut with unnerving
speed.

> Turn to **289**.

246

Using the Copper Key, you unlock the door and
hurry into the garden, not a moment too soon; as the
heavy door swings shut you hear crossbow bolts
ricocheting from the bands of studded iron.

The enclosed garden is filled with the fragrance of
exotic shrubs and trees, which cluster around a
sculptured pool of deep blue water. It is a beautiful
sight, but you dare not stop to enjoy it. The
Drakkarim and the palace guards know where you
are, and you must keep moving if you are to escape
them.

Beyond a tree-lined colonnade, a flight of steps ascends to a small portal in the wall of the upper palace. To your right, a leafy tunnel winds away into the trees and shrubs.

If you decide to climb the stairs to the small portal, turn to **352**.

If you would rather follow the winding path, turn to **391**.

If you possess the Kai Discipline of Tracking, turn to **220**.

247

The voyage through the Koos is breathtaking. The *Skyrider* glides between the towers of rock that rise from the valley floor with fantastic and unearthly grandeur. Far below, sulphurous water bubbles from fissures in the orange ground and streams of hissing lava carve circular channels, which glow like moats of liquid fire. You watch the sky but there are no signs of the enemy.

'Ikaresh,' says Banedon pensively. '"The Eagle's Lair". That is where we will find Tipasa the

Wanderer. It is the place of his birth and the home of his family. He roams the Dry Main but he always returns to Ikaresh.'

It is late afternoon when you reach the hills beyond the Koos that overlook the town of Ikaresh. Banedon moors the *Skyrider* to a pinnacle of stone, and a rope ladder is lowered to the ground. It has been decided that you and he will enter Ikaresh on foot and locate Tipasa, while Nolrim and the crew wait in hiding for you to return – the sight of the *Skyrider* hovering above the mountain town would be sure to arouse unwanted interest in your arrival.

You and Banedon prepare yourselves for your mission by staining your skins with brown copalla berries and dressing in the grey and white robes commonly worn by the mountain people of this region. Then you bid farewell to Nolrim and set off across the barren hills.

Pick a number from the *Random Number Table*.

If the number you have picked is 0–2, turn to **337**.
If it is 3–9, turn to **383**.

248

A small, heavy-set merchant is hawking his wares from a stall set close to the archway. His small beady eyes twinkle from beneath a ridiculously outsized turban. As you approach, he launches himself at you, desperately trying, with a flood of wild claims, to persuade you to buy his obviously inferior goods. He looks surprised when you interrupt him with your question. 'Tipasa?' he answers. 'Yes, I know where he lives.'

He holds up a gaudy waistcoat of pink and orange sackcloth and offers it to you. 'It would make a worthy gift for your esteemed friend,' he suggests, his eyes continually glancing at your belt pouch. 'Only 5 Gold Crowns, master.'

You realize you will first have to purchase this ridiculous garment before the merchant will tell you where Tipasa lives.

> If you wish to buy the waistcoat, pay the man 5 Gold Crowns, and turn to **328**.
> If you do not want to buy the waistcoat, or cannot afford to pay him 5 Gold Crowns, turn to **274**.

249

As the Vordak dies, its body gradually dissolves into a bubbling green liquid, shrivelling the plants that lie beneath the crumpled red robe. The swish of a sword alerts you to the Drakkarim who are now closing in around their slain leader. Without hesitation, you sheathe your weapon and rush for cover among the densely packed trees.

Turn to **228**.

250

As you watch the Kraan-riders disappear into the darkening sky, a roll of thunder rumbles across the plain from Barrakeesh. The sound is threatening and full of brooding menace, as if the city itself were cursing your escape.

You turn away and focus your attention on Banedon, your unexpected rescuer. The makeshift bandage that binds his wound is soaked with blood and he looks pale and weak.

If you have the Kai Discipline of Healing, turn to **377**.

If you do not have this skill, turn to **339**.

251

You are fortunate that you are not struck by the blast, but even so, the blue flame scorches your hand and arm and knocks you to the floor. Lose 6 ENDURANCE points.

If you are still alive, turn to **316**.

252

You whirl your feet away from the shining steel and narrowly escape being wounded as the axe bites inches deep into the polished stone floor. However, before the guard can strike another blow, you lash out and send the axe spinning from his hand. He screams, clutching broken fingers to his chest.

You turn and run towards an open door. The air is filled with the sound of pounding feet, for the palace guard are on full alert; together with the Drakkarim, they are now bent on finding and killing you as quickly as possible.

Beyond the door, a bridge rises at a slanted angle over an enclosed garden, joining this part of the palace to a needle-like tower of white marble. At the entrance to the bridge, a narrow stair disappears into the garden below.

If you wish to cross the bridge and enter the tower, turn to **396**.

If you decide to descend the stairs, turn to **215**.

253 – *Illustration XV (overleaf)*

Suddenly, the pain subsides; but a new horror is taking shape before your eyes. Out of the darkness, a green whorl of vapour is forming slowly into the shape of a glistening, serpent-like monster. A grey mist issues forth from the Darklord's mouth, floating towards the core of this horror, infusing it with the power of death. The serpent writhes and convulses as the grey mist fills its body, changing it from a dream-like illusion into a living nightmare. Two pinpoints of crimson glow from its eyes, as it slithers towards you.

Dhorgaan: COMBAT SKILL 20   ENDURANCE 40

If you possess a Jewelled Mace, you may add 5 to your COMBAT SKILL for the duration of the combat, for it is an enchanted weapon, especially effective against such a creature.

If you win the combat, turn to **335**.

XV. A green whorl of vapour is forming slowly into the shape of a glistening, serpent-like monster

254

The chill air whips past your face as you tumble towards Lake Inrahim. The Kraan-riders, the sky-ship and the distant horizon all melt into a kaleidoscope of shapes and images. You fear these will be the last things you will ever see.

You have prepared yourself for death and feel calm and relaxed. Suddenly, you feel your body engulfed by a mass of sticky fibres. There is a terrific jolt, which leaves you breathless and stunned. (Lose 2 ENDURANCE points.) The impossible is happening– you are no longer falling but rising!

You have been caught by a net of sticky strands like a fly in a web. You rise into the sky towards the flying ship as quickly as you fell. Three bearded dwarves clad in bright, padded battle-jerkins, pull you aboard an outrigger that runs the length of the hull. There is no time to express your gratitude for the small sky-ship is under attack from the Kraan-riders.

At the end of the outrigger, a dwarf is in hand-to-hand combat with a snarling Drakkar. He is losing the battle. As you rush to help him, another of the evil warriors lands in the centre of the craft, on top of the fortified platform.

If you wish to help the dwarf, turn to **280**.

If you wish to leap from the outrigger on to the fortified platform, turn to **361**.

255

As the Drakkar collapses to the ground, a Black Crystal Cube falls from his pocket. If you wish to take this item, place it in your own pocket and mark it on your *Action Chart* as a Special Item. The shriek of the Vordak drives you away from the dead body – his hideous cry is loud and very near.

Turn to **228**.

256

'Here you are,' says Banedon, flicking a Gold Crown into her empty bowl. 'Now will you help us in return?' She snatches the coin to her mouth and bites into the gold. Satisfied that the coin is real, she nods her head.

If you wish to ask her if she is Soushilla, turn to **307**.

If you wish to ask her if she knows where Tipasa the Wanderer can be found, turn to **314**.

257

The creature's curved beak gores your back, impaling you upon its razor-sharp tip. You are lifted into the air and dashed against the wall with one flick of the great bird's powerful neck. Mercifully, death is instantaneous as your skull is shattered against the hard, unyielding marble.

Your life and the hopes of Sommerlund end here.

258

The sun-sword tingles with power as you point it at the flame which hurtles nearer and nearer, its hiss becoming so loud that it drowns the noise of battle. You brace yourself for the moment of impact. The flame hits the Sommerswerd with a thunderous noise, and is held there in a ball of liquid purple fire that burns at the very tip of the magical blade. Instinctively, you whirl the Sommerswerd around your head and cast the fireball back into the sky.

The Vordak shrieks with terror but it is too late – its fate is sealed. The fire ball consumes the Zlanbeast and its rider in a massive explosion of sun-like brilliance.

Turn to **267**.

259

Two bolts whistle through the air and slam into your back. As pain tears through your body, you faint and fall on to the poison-tipped spikes. As your life's blood drains away, the last sound you hear is the hideous gloating laughter of Darklord Haakon rising above the ghoulish howl of his evil Drakkarim warriors.

Your life and the hopes of Sommerlund end here.

260

Using the cover of the excavation equipment scattered around the crater, you creep up on the sentry and empty the Tincture into the water flask resting by his feet.

A few minutes later, he reaches down and drinks from the flask. It is not long before he begins to feel very ill. As he staggers away to be violently sick, you slip into the Tomb unnoticed.

Turn to **395**.

261

You tumble earthwards, blurred colours flashing before your eyes. The Kraan-riders, the sky-ship and the distant horizon all melt into a kaleidoscope of shapes, the last images you see before smashing into the hard and barren salt-plain of Lake Inrahim.

Your life and the hopes of Sommerlund end here.

262

You have been detected; the Vordak shrieks a hideous high-pitched scream and points a bony finger towards your hiding place. Drakkarim crash through the undergrowth, cleaving a path with their black swords.

If you wish to draw your weapon and prepare for combat, turn to **212**.

If you wish to try to escape from them, turn to **393**.

263

The crone hobbles away into the dark alley; you and

Banedon retrace your steps to the eagle monolith, where an arrow sign points west to the main square. The evening shadows are lengthening as you set off from the eagle once more.

Turn to **216**.

264 – *Illustration XVI (overleaf)*

A terrible shriek rings out above the rush of the wind, filling your head with pain. You are being attacked by a powerful Mindblast. Unless you possess the Kai Discipline of Mindshield, deduct 2 ENDURANCE points from your current total.

The Itikar shudders and frantically twists its head from side to side as the shriek rings out again. You sense that the great bird is in agony, racked by the Mindblast. As you glance over your shoulder, your stomach becomes knotted with fear – a Kraan is swooping down to attack. On its back is your adversary: a Vordak, one of the undead and a hideous lieutenant of the Darklords. As the Kraan streaks towards you, the Vordak spreads its red-robed arms and leaps from the saddle. It lands behind you, astride the Itikar's back, its skeletal fingers sunk deep into your mount's feathered flesh. The shock of the impact throws you forward, and the reins slip from your hands.

The giant bird screeches in horror and pain as the Vordak's grip paralyses its spine. You must act quickly, for the Itikar is now plummeting towards the salt-plain of Lake Inrahim.

If you possess the Sommerswerd, turn to **315**.
If you do not possess this Special Item, turn to **299**.

XVI.   The Vordak lands behind you, astride the Itikar's back, its skeletal fingers sunk deep into your mount's feathered flesh

265

She refuses to say anything until you have placed some money in her begging bowl.

If you wish to give her a Gold Crown, make the adjustment to your *Action Chart*, and turn to **397**.

If you do not wish, or cannot afford, to give her any gold, turn to **256**.

266

Your Kai skill warns you that two palace guards are running up the spiral stairs from their guardroom in the base of the tower. Quickly, you ascend the stairs before the Drakkarim enter and see in which direction you have gone.

Turn to **322**.

267

The Drakkarim falter, blinded by the flash. Nolrim seizes the opportunity and urges his brethren forward against the invaders, leading the attack with his mighty battle-axe. Its razor edge whines and strikes sparks against the enemies' black armour, cutting through their unsteady ranks like a scythe through blighted corn.

You climb back on to the platform and see a Drakkar about to strike Banedon. The wizard seems unconcerned about the screaming warrior who threatens to decapitate him with a black broadsword. Banedon points his finger at the Drakkar, who is poised to strike.

If you wish to attack the Drakkar before he lands his blow upon Banedon's head, turn to **330**.

(continued over)

If you do not wish to attack, turn to **394**.

268

With the leap of a tiger, you snatch the glowing gem barely a second before Haakon's spiked fist slams into the floor where the jewel lay. You turn to face your enemy, the gem held high in your hand, its blue beam glinting on the Darklord's black armour. He shrinks beneath its glare and falls to his knees, a repulsive sucking noise issuing from his helm as he slowly begins to fade.

A sudden crack makes you start with shock, but you are no longer in danger. The glowing gem has vanished from your hand; like its master it has left this dimension, never to return.

Turn to **400**.

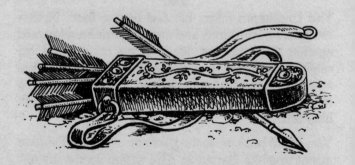

269

You stare at the drawbolt, willing it to move. The sound of running footsteps behind you sends a cold shiver down your spine as you realize that the Drakkarim are storming the stairs. Then, slowly, the drawbolt begins to move. As soon as it clears the bolt-hole, you pull open the stone portal and race through, unaware of what lies beyond.

Turn to **352**.

270

You race along the rock-strewn cave, eager to escape from the infected old man. The horrific stories that you have heard about vaxelus makes you careless in your haste, and you lose 2 Items from your Backpack. Choose which two Items to erase from your *Action Chart* (If you have no Backpack Items, you lose a Weapon and a Special Item instead.)

Turn to **241**.

271

The Kraan-rider screams past to your left, spun off course by your swift counter-blow. He is now over a hundred feet below, but is turning the Kraan for another attack. You wheel towards the south to avoid being caught between the two converging squadrons of Kraan-riders. Your change of direction increases the distance between you and your pursuers, but the Itikar is badly wounded and terrified by the shrieking Kraan.

You are close to despair; your feathered mount is losing a lot of blood, and could lapse into unconsciousness at any moment and drop you like a stone from the darkening sky. Suddenly you spot something in the distance – a sight that renews your faith in miracles.

Turn to **221**.

272

You follow a path along a dry gully, the bed of an ancient river that once flowed through the mountains. An arid breeze blows eddies of red dust along the banks of dead earth. The white-walled buildings of Ikaresh suddenly appear, and, as the dust settles, you find yourselves standing in a small square close to the open archway of the town's east gate.

Perched upon a tall basalt monolith in the centre of the square is an eagle – the emblem of this mountain town – cast in bronze. Three bronze arrows are held in its beak, each indicating an exit from the square.

If you wish to go north, towards the Dougga Market, turn to **376**.

If you wish to go west, towards the main square, turn to **216**.

If you wish to go south, along the Avenue of Eagles, turn to **342**.

273

The Akataz leaps through the air at your face. You fall backwards, kicking with both feet, but you are winded as the war-dog jolts the air from your lungs. It slashes your shoulder (lose 1 ENDURANCE point), before cartwheeling over the edge of the stairs, its howl cut short as it smashes into the marble floor of the lower palace.

You spring to your feet and draw your weapon, for the Drakkarim are running towards you. A terrible roar of hate and rage fills the hall: 'Kill him!' The

Drakkarim unsheathe their black swords, eager to obey their master's command. They attack you simultaneously.

Drakkarim: COMBAT SKILL 18   ENDURANCE 35

You can evade the combat at any time by running into the adjoining passage.

If you wish to evade combat, turn to **238**.
If you win the combat, turn to **345**.

274

Banedon holds a gleaming ring of silver beneath the merchant's nose and says, 'This is yours, my friend, if you tell us where Tipasa can be found.'

The merchant snatches the ring from the wizard's hand and stammers, 'The first alley on the left past the stables. He lives at the house with the blue door.'

You hurry across the crowded market place towards the stables and enter the street beyond. As you turn into the alley, you hear the merchant's shriek of dismay above the noise of the crowd; the ring has just dissolved on his finger. At the end of the alley you find the house with the blue door.

Turn to **206**.

275

You recognize the flag that flies above a fortified platform in the centre of this strange craft: it is the crescent and crystal star ensign of the Magicians' Guild of Toran, a city in northern Sommerlund. The sky-ship is commanded by a Sommlending wizard – one of your own countrymen. He is a blond-haired young man dressed in long, dark blue robes.

You are so stunned by the fateful appearance of the craft that you fail to notice the blood seeping from the Itikar's mouth: the creature is near to death. Suddenly, the great bird lets out a pitiful and agonizing caw. Its wings stiffen and its head falls limply forward as the last flicker of life escapes from its torn body. You are pitched forward and your stomach heaves as you plummet towards Lake Inrahim.

Pick a number from the *Random Number Table*.

If the number you have picked is *0–4*, turn to **374**.
If it is *5–8*, turn to **254**.
If it is *9*, turn to **261**.

276

'Why do you ask?' she replies suspiciously, blinking the tears from her eyes. 'What business do you have with Old Tipasa?'

'He is a friend,' replies Banedon, placing a Gold Crown on the tavern counter. The old woman covers the coin with her hand, her expression shrewd and calculating.

'Soushilla is old, her memory has faded with the passing years,' she says, waiting expectantly and glancing at Banedon's money pouch. He opens the flap to remove another Crown, but the pouch has been emptied by a nimble pickpocket. Sheepishly he avoids your stare, his face growing redder by the second.

'Five Gold Crowns may refresh my memory,' she says, her gaze now resting on you.

If you wish to pay the old woman 5 Gold Crowns, erase them from your *Action Chart* and turn to **326**.

If you do not have 5 Gold Crowns, or do not wish to give her the money, leave the tavern and turn to **202**.

277

You crouch low as you wait for your chance to leap up and open the door. More and more crossbow bolts ricochet from the wall and parapet every second. The sound of iron-shod boots sends a shiver down your spine; the Drakkarim are storming the stairs– it is now or never!

You spring to your feet and run to the door, grasping the iron drawbolt with trembling fingers. A steel-tipped missile splinters stone less than an inch from your hand, another ricochets and opens a cut above your eye. The instant the bolt clears the bolt-hole, you pull open the stone portal and race through, unaware of what lies beyond.

Turn to **352**.

278

You run, half-crouched, towards your golden blade, grab the hilt, and continue at full speed towards the cover of another pillar. Suddenly, a burst of energy leaps from the Darklord's fist, exploding into the base of the pillar, severing it from the floor. A tremendous roar fills your ears as you are thrown backwards by the shock of the blast. You lose 3 ENDURANCE points. Haakon's laugh rises above the crash of falling stone until your head is filled with an agonizing pain.

If you have the Kai Discipline of Mindshield, turn to **223**.

If you do not have this skill, turn to **379**.

279

A narrow corridor faces you, which is lit by the orange light of the setting sun filtering down from small open windows set high above in the patterned walls. The air is filled with the sound of running feet, for the Grand Palace is now on full alert. The palace guards and the evil Drakkarim are bent on finding and killing you, for their own lives will be forfeit if they fail.

You reach a door that opens on to an outside balcony. A stair descends to a bridge that connects a needle-like tower of white marble to the main palace. The stair itself continues past the bridge, disappearing down towards the palace gardens far below. You see no soldiers, either on the bridge or in the gardens.

If you wish to descend to the bridge and enter the marble tower, turn to **396**.

If you wish to continue past the bridge, descending the stairs to the palace gardens, turn to **215**.

280

The Drakkar is strangling the dwarf. As he catches sight of you, he releases his grip and smashes his mailed fist into the dwarf's face sending him tumbling into space. You are inflamed by this cold-blooded murder. You draw your weapon and attack.

Drakkar: COMBAT SKILL 18   ENDURANCE 25

Due to the speed of your attack, do not deduct any of your own ENDURANCE points in the first round of combat.

If you win the combat, turn to **213**.

281

As you turn to leave, the vaxeler bids you to wait. From a bundle of rags hidden beneath the bridge, he produces a gem-encrusted mace. The weapon is carved from solid silver and adorned with emeralds and diamonds along the haft. 'Take it, I beseech you, as a token of my eternal thanks.'

If you wish to accept this gift, mark the Jewelled Mace on your *Action Chart* as a Special Item (which you carry tucked into your belt) before leaving the cave.

Turn to **241**.

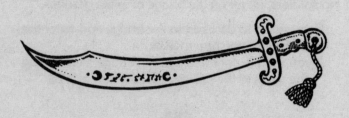

282

You leave the bell-tower and make your way down towards the sentry. At first, dodging from one turret to the next, it is easy to remain unseen. However, for the final thirty yards to the landing platform you will have no cover, for the platform and the palace roof are linked by an exposed gangplank. If you are to over-power the sentry, you must cross the gangplank undetected.

If you have the Kai Discipline of Mind Over Matter, turn to **295**.

If you do not possess this skill, pick a number from the *Random Number Table*. If you have the Kai Disciplines of either Hunting or Camouflage, add 2 to the number you have picked. If you have reached the Kai rank of Warmarn or higher, add 3.

> If your total score is now *0–4*, turn to **357**.
> If your total is *5–9*, turn to **389**.
> If your total is *10* or more, turn to **236**.

283

The dwarves are not offended by your refusal. They have seen men stirred to fury or laid unconscious by a jug of Bor-brew. Nolrim grasps the tankard and downs the draught with one awesome gulp, removing the froth from his ginger beard with a practised flick of his forefinger.

> If you wish to ask the dwarves how they came to be under Banedon's command, turn to **291**.
> If you wish to bid them goodnight, turn to **359**.

284

You call out to them to stop, but your accent merely confirms their suspicions that you are a spy. A rock hurtles through the air and gashes your forehead. You lose 3 ENDURANCE points. 'Run, Lone Wolf!' screams Banedon. 'They will cut you to pieces!'

As they race nearer, the crazed look in their eyes quickly tells you it would be madness to stay. You turn and run for all you are worth.

Turn to **340**.

285 – *Illustration XVII (overleaf)*

As you turn and sprint along the passage, a terrible roar of hatred and rage fills the hall: 'Kill him!'

XVII.   In a flash of light the Drakkar is gone

You glance back. The Drakkarim are unsheathing their black swords, eager to obey their master's command. You race down some stairs, through a silver archway, and along a balcony that overlooks the lower palace.

The Akataz is nearly upon you; you feel its fetid breath on your legs. Instinctively, you dodge aside at the very second it leaps. It crashes muzzle-first into a marble pillar. A howl of pain leaves its broken mouth as you step forward and strike a death blow; it will never attack again.

You glimpse the grim silhouette of Darklord Haakon in the hall below, his spiked fist raised. A Drakkar appears as if from nowhere and advances, a sword held high above his skull-like helm. There is a deafening crack as a bolt of blue lightning streaks from a stone in the Darklord's hand, and comes hurtling towards you. The Drakkar lunges and wounds your arm (you lose 2 ENDURANCE points), but he now stands in the path of the bolt. In a flash of light, the Drakkar is gone, leaving only cinders and the rotten odour of scorched flesh behind.

At the end of the balcony is another arch and a staircase.

If you wish to escape through the arch, turn to **381**.
If you wish to escape by the stairs, turn to **317**.

286

As night falls, your desperate quest begins. The Giaks pose few problems that you cannot overcome with your warrior skills, for they have been overworked to the point of exhaustion. Only the Drakkarim show

287

any sign of vigilance, but even then, there are less than a dozen patrolling the entire crater. Not until you reach the main entrance to the Tomb do you encounter any real difficulty.

A Drakkar stands on guard, his cruel eyes glinting behind his twisted iron death-mask. Occasionally, he diverts his attention from the watch to take a drink from a water flask.

If you have the Kai Discipline of Mind Over Matter, turn to **214**.
If you do not have this skill, turn to **239**.

287

Itikar are by nature wild and malicious creatures, and it can take many years for a rider to tame and train one. However, the effort is well worthwhile as once this has been accomplished, the giant black birds are fiercely loyal.

The Itikar senses that you are not his master and tries to drive you away, wounding your back with a glancing blow from its powerful beak. You lose 1 ENDURANCE point. However, due to sheer strength of will, you manage to climb into the saddle and subdue the creature. It turns its head and fixes you with a cold black stare, but you sense that it is now no longer hostile.

Suddenly, you catch sight of the Drakkarim, streaming across the gangplank. You stretch forward, unhook the Itikar's anchor rope from the saddle ring and grab the thick leather reins.

Turn to **343**.

288

The Drakkar curses you with his dying breath, his cry fading as he falls from the platform. You rush to aid your wounded countryman, but the battle is not yet over. A Kraan-rider is swooping towards you, a crossbow levelled at your head; he fires and the bolt shoots towards your face. Then a shrill, metallic whine rings in your ears as the bolt miraculously ricochets away, deflected by an invisible shield.

If you possess a Crystal Star Pendant, turn to **399**.
If you do not have this Special Item, turn to **294**.

289

The throne begins to revolve. A terrible howling fills your ears, changing almost instantaneously to the growling of a harsh gutteral language, the like of which you have never heard before. Words and sounds that the mouths of men could never be shaped to speak roll through the chamber like thunder. It is the dark tongue, spoken by Haakon, Lord of Aarnak, Darklord of Helgedad.

He rises from the throne, the ghastly voice still echoing from his unnatural mouth. A spiked fist opens to reveal a glowing stone; blue flame smoulders around its surface and you can feel the currents of power that radiate from its core. Suddenly, his words change and you hear a tongue you know so well – Sommlending.

'Look on your doom, Kai Lord!'

There is a deafening crack, a surge of power, and a fireball of blue flame hurtles towards your head.

If you possess the Sommerswerd, turn to **311**.
If you do not have this Special Item, turn to **219**.

290

You search the body of the dead Drakkar leader and discover in his pocket a Black Crystal Cube. If you wish to keep the Black Crystal Cube, place it in your pocket and mark it on your *Action Chart* as a Special Item.

The sound of more Drakkarim thundering down the tower stairs prompts you to leave the other bodies and hurry over to the wooden door.

Turn to **246**.

291

You learn that the dwarves were once the crew of a more conventional vessel, a merchantman that sailed the Tentarias of southern Magnamund. The Tentarias are a vast expanse of lakes and land-locked seas, which connect to form a continuous canal stretching over a thousand miles. They were created, as was the Rymerift of Durenor, by a massive land-slide. Three years ago, the dwarves' former captain, a dwarf named Quan, lost his ship, cargo and crew whilst gambling at cards; it seems the unfortunate captain was unaware of Banedon's true profession until it was far too late. As a result Banedon became the dwarves' captain, and ever since they have adventured with him across the lands and skies of southern Magnamund. The *Skyrider* itself was given to Banedon by the Magicians of Dessi, in return for his help in defeating the Gagadoth – a monstrous creature that terrorized their land, and over which their own sorcery could not prevail.

The *Skyrider* was travelling from Dessi on its way to Barrakeesh when you appeared. The dwarves have overheard your talk with Banedon and are excited by the prospect of a new adventure. They seem undaunted by the deadly dangers that it will certainly involve.

Turn to **359**.

292

Your Kai sense tells you that the house at the end of the alleyway is Tipasa's home. You signal to Banedon to follow as you approach the blue door.

Turn to **206**.

293

For a moment, your sense of bearing is completely lost as you tumble and spin into the void, unaware of what is happening to your body. You try to cry out, but your cries are lost on the wind as it rushes past. You hit the upper branches of a toa tree. You are stunned by the crash, and your body becomes numb.

By the time your broken body is found by the Drakkarim, you have bled to death.

Your life and the hopes of Sommerlund end here.

294

You see the young magician lower his staff, a trace of a smile on his pain-racked face.

'Alas, I was too slow to shield myself,' he says wryly, as you kneel at his side and free the spear that pins him to the floor. The wound is serious, and you hastily staunch the bleeding with strips of cloth torn from his dark blue robes.

The wizard then introduces himself. 'I am Banedon, Journeymaster to the Guild of the Crystal Star,' he says, his voice weak and shaky. 'However, you need not introduce yourself, Lone Wolf, for only you would attract such company this far from home.' He glances at the Kraan-riders swooping past the sky-ship on every side. 'Help me to my feet – we must escape before they drag us from the sky.'

You support the wizard as he grasps the ship's helm – a radiant crystal sphere with hundreds of glowing facets set upon a slim silver rod.

No sooner has his hand closed around the crystal than there is a tremendous explosion.

Turn to **323**.

295

Focusing your skill upon a money pouch that hangs from the sentry's belt, you concentrate on untying the leather thong that secures it. Seconds later, the pouch drops to the ground and spills its contents. The guard yelps in horror as he sees his gold rolling over the edge of the platform and drops to his knees to gather what little remains. As he turns his back, you break cover and run across the gangplank.

Turn to **236**.

296

Inside, the eating house is full of townsfolk, all seated at small stone tables. Ornate hubble-bubble pipes add to the colourful atmosphere as the smokers discuss all kinds of matters. A quarrelsome trio of Ikareshi are lamenting the death of the old Zakhan, others give voice to various grievances, calling their new leader an ox, a brute and other such names. In your opinion, they speak too highly of him. Two rough-faced Ikareshi bid you welcome and invite you to share their pipe.

If you wish to accept their offer, turn to **362**.

If you wish to decline, you can leave the eating-house and continue along the avenue, and turn to **388**.

297

The guards are the first to recover from the surprise of the encounter. They attack, opening a deep wound in your chest. Lose 4 ENDURANCE points.

If you are still alive, and wish to fight the guards, turn to **334**.

If you wish to try to escape by running back up the stairs, turn to **209**.

298

You are trying to decide whether to try prising open the door, when you hear the sound of stone grating on stone. The door slowly opens to reveal a large chamber. It is dimly lit but in the thick dust which covers the marble floor you can see innumerable footprints.

Then, as you enter, you catch sight of a rough stone throne, facing the wall on the far side of the chamber. Behind you, the stone door slides shut with unnerving speed.

Turn to **289**.

299

The Vordak removes a bony hand, drenched in blood, from the Itikar's back and claws at a black iron mace hanging from its belt. It raises the weapon and lunges at your head. It is impossible to evade its attack; you must fight the creature to the death.

Vordak: COMBAT SKILL 17   ENDURANCE 25

Unless you have the Kai Discipline of Mindshield, deduct 2 points from your COMBAT SKILL for the duration of this fight, for the Vordak is attacking you with its Mindforce. It is immune to Mindblast.

If you win the fight, turn to **203**.

300

You awake shortly after dawn to the sound of snoring dwarves and the low hum of the *Skyrider*. Gathering your equipment, you climb on deck to find everything in shadow, for the *Skyrider* is hovering beneath a massive outcrop of sandstone that juts out from the side of a mountain, thousands of feet above the valley floor below. Banedon stands at the helm, but he is no longer in a trance.

'Kraan-riders,' he says, pointing to the sun-bleached valley beyond the shadows. 'They arrived with the dawn.'

You stare out across this alien landscape, a mountain valley filled with pillars of massive and precariously balanced boulders. The Vassagonians call this place the Koos – 'the needles'. The rocky columns reach so high into the sky that an avalanche seems unavoidable. Perched upon two of the columns are Kraan, their Drakkar riders scouring the valley with telescopes. An hour passes before they take to the air and disappear.

'Trim the boomsails, bo'sun Nolrim,' orders Banedon, his voice barely audible above the increasing hum of the *Skyrider*. 'We've a fast run ahead.'

If you possess a Black Crystal Cube, turn to **229**.
If you do not have this Special Item, turn to **247**.

301

Using the bands of iron as footholds, you clamber to the top of the door. Long spikes protrude from the timber crossbar, each coated with an oily black tar. Just as you are stepping over the spikes, the guards fire their crossbows.

Pick a number from the *Random Number Table*. If you have reached the Kai rank of Guardian or higher, subtract 2 from the number you have picked. If you have the Kai Discipline of Hunting, subtract 1 from this number.

If your total score is below 4, turn to **363**.
If your score is 5–9, turn to **259**.

302

Banedon takes over the helm as his extraordinary ship, the *Skyrider*, as the dwarves call it, speeds through the gathering darkness towards the Dahir Pass. Visibility diminishes with each passing minute until, finally, you can see no further than the outriggers. You feel uneasy; if the *Skyrider* veers but a fraction off course, you will be smashed to pieces against the mountainside.

'Do not worry, Lone Wolf,' says Nolrim, the dwarf with the velvet satchel. 'The Captain will see us through.'

Banedon stands with his hand resting lightly on the glowing crystal, relaxed as if in a trance. His eyes are closed and a crackle of energy, like fine white lightning, traces an intricate pattern over his forehead and temples.

The dwarf leads you to the cabin at the rear of the craft where the crew are excitedly recounting their victory over the Kraan-riders. They are seated about a table cluttered with plates of steaming food and jugs of foaming ale. The rich smell of spiced meat and Bor-brew fills your nostrils, reminding you of how ravenously hungry you are.

You make short work of the meat and marrow placed before you. Restore 3 ENDURANCE points. However, you are unsure about accepting a jug of ale; Bor-brew is so strong, that in many cities of Magnamund it has been banned for fear of the havoc it can cause.

If you wish to accept a jug of the notorious ale, turn to **392**.

If you decide to decline the offer, turn to **283**.

303

With speed and stealth you approach the sentry from behind, and silence him for good with a sharp twist of the neck. You drag the body away and cover it with a wheelbarrow before entering the Tomb.

Turn to **395**.

304

The Vordak collapses at your feet, but before you can escape, you are surrounded by Drakkarim. A silence fills the arboretum; all is deathly quiet. You prepare to cut your way out but more of the evil warriors appear. You shiver with the chill of fear – the Drakkarim reinforcements are armed with heavy bronze crossbows.

As you shout your battle cry 'For Sommerlund!' you are hit by a volley of poison-tipped bolts, which hurl you backwards to the soft earth. The last sound you hear as your life's blood drains away into the soil is the hideous gloating laughter of Darklord Haakon, rising above the ghoulish howl of his Drakkarim.

Your life and the hopes of Sommerlund end here.

305

Tying one end of the rope to the parapet rail, you drop the other end over the side and glissade down the tower. You have reached half-way when you see two Drakkarim above you, sawing at the knot. Suddenly, the rope snaps and you plummet into the void.

Pick a number from the *Random Number Table*.

If the number you have picked is *0–2*, turn to **293**.
If it is *3–9*, turn to **234**.

306 – *Illustration XVIII*

'Hold tight, Lone Wolf,' shouts Banedon, as he regains control of the glowing crystal helm. You obey, and grasp the parapet rail, bracing your feet against a deck cleat for safety, for you have guessed what manoeuvre the young wizard is about to perform.

'Pirate roll!' he shouts to his fighting dwarves, and

XVIII.   'Pirate roll!' he shouts to the fighting dwarves

jerks the helm to the left. The *Skyrider* reponds to his touch, swerving violently as the deck swings from a horizontal to a near-vertical angle. The dwarves heed his cry and throw themselves to the deck, clutching the boards like limpets to a galleon's keel.

The Drakkarim are caught off-balance and hurtle over the decks and outriggers, tumbling into the void. Banedon rights the craft and a victory cheer resounds across the decks as you speed away into the Koos. 'Blood for blood!'

Turn to **247**.

307

'Yes, yes. I am Soushilla,' she replies.

'Do you know where we can find Tipasa the Wanderer?' asks Banedon.

The old crone does not reply, she merely holds out her begging bowl in expectation. Banedon loses another crown before she answers his question.

Turn to **314**.

308

It can take many years for a rider to tame an Itikar, for by nature they are wild and malicious creatures. You use your Kai skill to communicate with the giant bird, to assure it that you mean no harm. It fixes you with a cold, black stare, but you sense that it is no longer hostile.

As you settle in its wide saddle, you catch sight of the Drakkarim as they stream across the gangplank.

Quickly you lean forward, unhook the anchor rope from the saddle ring and grab the thick leather reins.

Turn to **343**.

309

As you enter the stables, you are overpowered by the smell of the douggas. You grit your teeth and cover your nose with your robe. A small boy sniggers at your reaction and says, 'You're not Ikareshi – I can tell.' He mimics your grimace, exposing a line of broken teeth.

'Do you know where Tipasa the Wanderer lives?' asks Banedon, holding up a silver ring. The boy's eyes nearly pop out of his head at the sight of the gleaming silver.

'Oh yes, yes, yes I do indeed,' he stammers in his excitement. 'Walk up the street and take the first passage on your left. The old wanderer lives at the house with the blue door.'

Banedon flicks the ring into the air and the urchin catches it in his grubby hands. You hurry away from the stables and begin to search for the passageway. Just as you find it, you hear the young boy shriek with disappointment; the ring has just dissolved on his finger. At the end of the rubbish-strewn alley you find the house with the blue door.

Turn to **206**.

310

As you climb over the lifeless bodies, you notice a Copper Key on a chain around one of their necks.

Grabbing the Key, you slip it into your pocket, and race down the steps towards a dim light below. Mark the Copper Key on your *Action Chart* as a Special Item.

A small fire, over which is roasting a chicken on a spit, illuminates a guard room at the base of the tower. On the back of a wrought-iron chair hangs a Canteen of Water, and lying beside it is a razor-sharp Broadsword. You may take either of these items if you wish, and mark them on your *Action Chart* (the Canteen is a Backpack Item).

You hear the Drakkarim rushing down the tower stairs. They will soon be upon you.

> If you wish to leave the tower by a door in the north wall, turn to **246**.
> If you wish to prepare yourself for combat and wait for the Drakkarim to appear, turn to **231**.

311

You raise your golden sword just in time to deflect the bolt of raw energy. It screams from your blade and explodes into the chamber wall, gouging a hole several feet deep in the steel-hard rock. The impact jars the Sommerswerd from your hand; the blade arcs through the dust-choked air and embeds itself, upright, in the stone floor. You roll across the floor and take cover behind a pillar.

'Your doom, Kai Lord,' spits Haakon, 'is but seconds away.'

If you wish to try to retrieve the Sommerswerd, turn to **278**.

If you wish to try to move to a new hiding place, under cover of the swirling dust, turn to **350**.

If you wish to stay where you are, turn to **230**.

312

The dwarves are clearing the deck of battle debris. A dead Drakkar lies sprawled face down across a pile of chests and sacks roped beneath the boomsail. As the dwarves grab his legs to cast him over the side he suddenly springs to life, sending the dwarves tumbling in all directions. He screams like a fiend, his black axe cutting a wide arc around his blood-smeared body. A curse, vile and evil, echoes from his death-mask as he draws back the axe to throw. His target is you.

If you have the Kai Discipline of Hunting or Sixth Sense, turn to **210**.

If you have neither of these skills, pick a number from the *Random Number Table*.

If the number you have picked is *0–4*, turn to **354**.
If it is *5–8*, turn to **371**.
If it is *9*, turn to **232**.

313

Below the bell-tower you see a line of Itikar pens, each with its own circular landing platform. Itikar are a breed of huge black birds that nest in eyries high in the peaks of the Dahir and Vakar mountains. The Vassagonians have long since tamed these giants of the skies, using them as winged mounts for their army leaders, their scouts, couriers and envoys.

An Itikar and rider swoop down out of the reddening sky and alight upon the platform nearest to the bell-tower. Slaves hurl a rope to the rider, who in turn fixes it to a saddle ring before he jumps to the ground. The Itikar caws and beats its huge wings as it is slowly winched into the pen by a hidden capstan.

The rider and the slaves leave the platform; there is now only one sentry on guard at the pen. If you can overpower him, you can make your escape on the back of the giant bird.

If you possess a Blowpipe and Sleep Dart, turn to **325**.

If you do not have these Items, turn to **282**.

314

'Tipasa can be found at the main square – he is always there at this time of day,' cringes the woman, her face creased into an exaggerated smile.

If you have the Kai Discipline of Sixth Sense, turn to **358**.

If you do not possess this skill, turn to **263**.

315

As you unsheathe the Sommerswerd, a vivid golden

flame shoots along the blade. The Vordak shrieks in terror, its blood-drenched bony fingers clawing at a black iron mace that hangs from its belt. It raises the mace to parry your blow, but the sun-sword shears through the iron, a splash of blue flame erupting in its wake. You strike again, curving the golden blade in a great arc. It bites into the Vordak's neck, tearing through its unnatural body, and severing it diagonally from collar bone to hip. A sickening acidic smell chokes your throat as a fountain of green slime erupts from beneath the red robe. The Vordak crumples and topples from view, its dissolving corpse hissing as it spirals towards Lake Inrahim.

Sheathing your sword, you grab the reins and fight to control your injured mount. You have slain the Vordak but the battle is not yet won. The Itikar is losing a lot of blood; it could become unconscious at any moment and drop like a stone.

Suddenly you spot something in the distance. It is a sight that renews your faith in miracles.

Turn to **221**.

316

You stagger to your feet to see the *Skyrider* being engulfed by Drakkarim; they leap from their shrieking Kraan and crash on to the decks and outriggers, their black swords already drawn from their scabbards. The dwarves are caught by surprise, their weapons have been unloaded and stored below deck. Even so, they are quick to rally and fight with skill and fury. Above the din you hear Nolrim's joyous battle-cry, 'Blood for blood!'

An unexpected blow catches you squarely on the back, knocking you from the platform to the deck below. You have risen to one knee when your assailant attacks again. You cannot evade him.

Drakkar: COMBAT SKILL 18   ENDURANCE 26

Due to the surprise of the attack, reduce your COMBAT SKILL by 2 for the first 3 rounds of combat.

If you win the combat, turn to **333**.

317

The blood is pounding in your ears as you bound up the marble steps. Twenty feet ahead of you, there is a landing with a stone door set into the wall. The stairs continue to ascend to a parapeted walkway, at the end of which is another stone door, identical to the first. Suddenly, the door on the first landing swings open and a palace guard wheels round to face you.

'Majhan!' he cries, fumbling for the hilt of his sword.

If you wish to attack the guard before he draws his weapon, turn to **338**.

If you wish to barge him aside and continue climbing the stairs, turn to **372**.

318

'Ah, Tipasa,' he replies thoughtfully. 'He lives near the Dougga Market, but exactly where his home is I am not sure . . . I haven't seen old Tipasa for years. If you should find him, remind him of Khamsin the Goatherd. He still owes me twelve Crowns – that I have not forgotten.' You thank the goatherd for his help and bid him farewell before continuing your trek to Ikaresh.

Turn to **272**.

319

The Onyx Medallion is beginning to glow and vibrate in your pocket. This Special Item, torn from the armour of a renegade Vassagonian captain during the battle of Ruanon, enables you to communicate with the Itikar. You reassure it that you mean no harm. Itikar are by nature wild and malicious, creatures, but the power of the Onyx Medallion tames this natural instinct, subduing them to the wearer's command.

As you settle in the wide saddle, you catch sight of the Drakkarim streaming across the gangplank. Quickly, you lean forward, unhook the Itikar's anchor rope from the saddle ring and grab the thick leather reins.

Turn to **343**.

320

Dawn is breaking on the horizon of a low hill, blurred and dotted with small tufted trees. Swiftly the

Skyrider has voyaged through the night to arrive at the foothills of the Koneshi mountains, in whose folds the sky-ship is safely tucked away from watchful eyes. Twenty-five miles to the north, across a landscape of barren rock and dry brush, lies the Tomb of the Majhan.

You and Banedon set off before the dawn, anxious not to waste either time or the protective cover of darkness. Now, as the great golden disc of the sun rises in the sky, for the first time you can see your goal. A massive excavation has exposed the heart of this scorched land, delving deep around the tombs of its forgotten ancestors. Thousands of Giaks, spiteful and malicious servants of the Darklords, labour unceasingly to remove rock and sand from this quarry, forced by Drakkarim to drag their back-breaking loads up ramps to the rim of the crater.

Close to the edge of the crater, an encampment of black tents surrounds a large domed canopy. Lying in the shade of this construction is a huge flying creature – an Imperial Zlanbeast. Its presence here can only mean one thing: Darklord Haakon has arrived. The thought chills your blood but you draw comfort from the labour of his slaves. That they continue to labour is a sign that their mission has yet to be completed: the *Book of the Magnakai* has yet to be found.

It is impossible to approach the crater unseen; you will have to wait for darkness before you attempt to enter the Tomb. During your long wait, it is agreed that Banedon should attempt to find Tipasa. It is likely that he is being held captive inside the encampment–

the Darklords would be unlikely to kill him before discovering the treasure they seek.

During the day, you must eat a Meal or lose 3 ENDURANCE points. Make the necessary adjustments to your *Action Chart*.

Turn to **286**.

321

You place the Oede herb upon the stone bridge and step back. At first the vaxeler is suspicious and frightened – nobody has dared to enter his cave for many years. But when he recognizes the golden leaves of the Oede herb, he breaks down, weeping tears of joy.

'May the Majhan bless you – may you live in eternal peace,' he cries, his feeble voice brimming over with emotion. 'How can I ever repay this kindness?'

If you wish to question the vaxeler about Tipasa the Wanderer, turn to **356**.

(continued over)

If you wish to leave the cave and press on towards Ikaresh, turn to **281**.

322

The stairs are high and steep. You gasp for breath and force your aching legs to climb, for the Drakkarim are less than a dozen steps behind you. At the top of the tower, an open arch leads out on to a platform where a huge kettledrum stands. This is used by the tower guard to send messages to the other palace towers. A bleached hide is stretched across its surface and a black wooden beater hangs from the side.

If you wish to push the drum down the tower stairs, turn to **329**.

If you prefer to ignore the drum and escape out on to the platform, turn to **387**.

323 – *Illustration XIX*

The explosion is followed by a huge cloud of smoke, which engulfs a cabin perched on the rear deck. As the noise rumbles across the desolate salt-plain, you hear the agonizing shriek of a wounded Kraan, it spirals past the platform, a ragged hole rent in its broken wing.

The smoke clears to reveal the grinning face of a dwarf at the cabin window. A smear of soot blackens his rosy cheeks and exaggerates the whiteness of his crooked teeth. He is holding a tube of smoking steel that you assume to be a magic staff, until you notice that each of the dwarf crew carry identical staves. As they point them at the swooping Kraan, gouts of smoke and flame bellow from their tips. Suddenly you recognize the weapons and their wielders— they

XIX.   The smoke clears to reveal the grinning face of a dwarf at the cabin window

are dwarves from the mountain kingdom of Bor, armed with one of the inventions for which these ingenious artisans are justly famous throughout Magnamund.

The Kraan are terrified by the noise; they turn their leathery tails and fly away, their Drakkar riders powerless to stop them. The primitive guns have claimed only one victim, but nevertheless, they have driven off the enemy and saved the sky-ship from disaster.

Banedon steers the craft about, banking steeply until the ship faces the darkening peaks of the southern mountains and the distinct V-shaped cleft of the Dahir Pass.

Pick a number from the *Random Number Table*.

If the number you have picked is *0–2*, turn to **250**.
If it is *3–9*, turn to **312**.

324

You are less than ten feet from the sentry when he senses that something is wrong. He turns to confront you just as you are making your attack.

Drakkar Sentry: COMBAT SKILL 18   ENDURANCE 25

If you win the combat, hide the body and enter the tomb.

Turn to **395**.

325

Taking care to load the Blowpipe correctly, you raise the unfamiliar weapon to your lips and take aim. The sentry is standing very still; he makes a perfect target. You inflate your cheeks and fire.

Pick a number from the *Random Number Table*. If you have the Kai Discipline of Weaponskill (any weapon), add 2 to the number you have picked.

If your total is now *0–3*, turn to **384**.
If your total is now *4* or more, turn to **398**.

326

'Walk along the street to the Dougga Market. Behind the stables there is an alley. Tipasa lives there, in the house with the blue door.'

As you make your way through the dancing crowd to the tavern door, you take care to keep both hands on your belt pouch. An embarrassed Banedon follows in your footsteps, cursing his misfortune under his breath.

Turn to **202**.

327

Your blow has opened a wide gash in both the Drakkar and his mount. The Kraan spins uncontrollably, discarding its black-clad rider as it spirals earthwards. With the terrible cries of the doomed Drakkar fading below, you wheel to the south to avoid being caught between the two converging squadrons of Kraan-riders.

The quick change of direction increases the distance between you and your pursuers, but the Itikar is badly wounded and you are close to despair; your mount is losing so much blood that it could lapse into unconsciousness at any moment, dropping you like a stone on to Lake Inrahim.

Suddenly, you spot something in the distance. It is a sight that renews your faith in miracles.

Turn to **221**.

328

The merchant's face beams with joy as he pockets your gold. Deduct this from your *Action Chart*.

'The first alley on the left past the stables,' he says. 'He lives in the house with the blue door.'

You hurry across the crowded market-place towards the stables and enter the street beyond. As you turn into the rubbish-strewn alley, you see the blue door facing you at the end of the passage.

Turn to **206**.

329

The heavy copper drum rolls from its wooden base and crashes down the tower stair, a thunderous boom echoing from the dark as it careers on a collision course with the enemy. The screams of horror are cut short as the drum hurtles through the ranks of the Drakkarim, crushing them into the hard stone steps.

Your quick action has scattered your pursuers, but victory turns sour when you discover that you are trapped; there are no other stairs from the platform. You have delayed the Drakkarim but your reprieve is only temporary.

If you possess a rope, you can attempt to climb down to the gardens below. Turn to **305**.

If you do not possess a Rope, turn to **387**.

330

You parry the Drakkar's blow and turn it aside, but he is quick to recover. He turns to face you and bellows a vile curse, his broadsword arcing back towards your skull.

Drakkar: COMBAT SKILL 18   ENDURANCE 23

If you win the combat and it lasts for 2 rounds or less, turn to **243**.

If the combat lasts more than 2 rounds, turn to **394**.

331

You have little sleep that night as you lie thinking about the quest that lies before you, haunted by the fear that the Darklords may already have found the *Book of the Magnakai*.

You rise before dawn and breakfast on a meal of sheep's butter and dried milk cake, before bidding farewell to Tipasa's wife. The trek back to the *Skyrider* passes uneventfully, and by noon you have reached the rocky crag where the craft is moored. Nolrim is the first to greet you, but he cannot hide his disappointment that you have returned unaccompanied.

'Do not worry – the answer lies here,' says Banedon, holding up Tipasa's diary. 'Prepare to set sail.'

As the *Skyrider* rises into the clear blue sky, Banedon hands over the helm to Nolrim and bids you follow him to his quarters at the prow. For three hours he pours over his charts, making calculations, checking instrument readings and racking his brain for the solution that will pinpoint the Tomb of the Majhan.

'It's no use,' he says, tired and exasperated. 'I cannot fathom these numbers.'

As you peer at the pages of Tipasa's diary, suddenly you realize that they are written in code. What Banedon had assumed to be the positions of stars are a code to three numbers that give the precise location of the Tomb.

Consult the map at the front of this book to help you discover the location of the Tomb of the Majhan.

The first of the three numbers is equal to the number of oases on the trail between Ikaresh and Bir Rabalou. The second number is equal to the number of cities in Vassagonia. The third number is equal to the number of islands off the coast of Cape Kabar.

When you have broken the code, write the numbers in order and turn to the entry number that they indicate.

332

Leaving the arbour, you press on towards the outer wall of the arboretum. Through the dense foliage you can make out a narrow, arched doorway that leads to an open chamber. A stairway ascends to a parapeted walkway, at the end of which is a stone door. You are half-way up the stairs when the sound of a crossbow being cocked freezes your blood. To turn back now would be suicide; you grit your teeth and bound up the stairs as a hail of crossbow fire slams into the steps on either side of you.

Turn to **372**.

333

You catch a glimpse of Nolrim fighting his way through a mass of red-cloaked Drakkarim, his two-handed battle axe bringing down three of them in as many blows. He cuts a path to your side and points with his blood-stained axe to a creature hovering high above the *Skyrider*.

You recognize it to be a Zlanbeast, a creature rather like a Kraan but far larger than its leathery sub-species. Upon its back sits a red-robed Vordak, a staff of black iron in its skeletal hand. There is a flash and a stream of liquid blue flame pours from its tip.

It you possess the Sommerswerd, turn to **258**.
If you do not have this Special Item, turn to **348**.

334

You are in combat with two grim-faced warriors. They block the stairs and you must fight both of them as one enemy.

Tower Guards: COMBAT SKILL 17   ENDURANCE 32

If you wish to avoid combat at any time by running back up the spiral staircase, turn to **209**.
If you win the fight, turn to **310**.

335

As you strike the death blow, the Dhorgaan shimmers and winks out of existence. Darklord Haakon reels back as if weakened by the death of his creation. The glowing stone falls from his hand and rolls across the chamber, coming to rest midway between you.

If you wish to attempt to grab the stone, turn to **268**.
If you wish to ignore the stone and attack Haakon, turn to **390**.
If you have the Kai Discipline of Sixth Sense, turn to **204**.

336

Standing at a fortified platform in the centre of the strange craft, is a blond-haired young man with deep, brooding eyes. Instantly you recognize him: it is Banedon, the young Sommlending magician who gave you the Crystal Star Pendant at the ruins of Raumas, after you had saved his life in a Giak ambush.

You are so stunned by his unexpected appearance that you fail to notice the blood seeping from the Itikar's mouth; the creature is near to death. Suddenly, the great bird lets out a pitiful and agonized caw, its wings stiffen and its head falls limp as the last flicker of life escapes from its torn body. It pitches you forward and your stomach heaves as you plummet towards Lake Inrahim.

Pick a number from the *Random Number Table*.

If the number you have picked is *0–4*, turn to **374**.
It it is *5–8*, turn to **254**.
If it is *9*, turn to **261**.

337

Without the breeze of the speeding *Skyrider* to cool you, the heat of the mountains is almost unbearable. You trudge across the loose reddish sand, your faces covered to keep the dust from choking your throats. All that seems to grow in this desolate waste is the wire-hard grass that tears at your boots and leggings.

As you reach the outskirts of Ikaresh, you pass a small, round hut where a goat is eating from a manger by the door. A man appears at the darkened doorway and bids you welcome; he touches his forehead in a salute of friendship and invites you both to enter his humble home.

If you wish to accept his invitation, turn to **225**.

If you wish to decline his offer and continue towards Ikaresh, turn to **272**.

If you have the Kai Discipline of Sixth Sense, turn to **365**.

338

Using your skill for unarmed combat taught to you by your Kai masters, you grab the startled guard by the throat and pitch him over the low wall at the edge of the landing. His cry of terror fills the air until he crashes into the flagstones below.

If you wish to continue climbing the stairs towards the door of the walkway, turn to **372**.

If you wish to enter the door through which the guard came, turn to **279**.

339

Two dwarves clamber on to the platform and hurry to their young captain's side. One flicks open a red velvet satchel strapped to his barrel-like chest, and removes a glass vial and a clean linen bandage. They attend to the wound, and, as his strength returns, Banedon listens intently to your account of the terrifying events that have led up to this meeting. As you conclude your woeful tale, Banedon speaks, his voice full of grim determination.

'The future of Sommerlund rests in our hands, Lone Wolf. We must stop Darklord Haakon from destroying the *Book of the Magnakai*. I have heard tell of the

Tomb of the Majhan from the nomads of the Dry Main. They say it is a terrible place, a place of horror and death – for what little there is left to die there. It lies beyond the Dahir, near the oasis of Bal-loftan. That is all I know, for the Majhan hid their tombs well and what few traces remained have long since disappeared beneath the shifting sands of the Dry Main.'

Your face conveys the disappointment you feel on hearing these words.

'However, all is not lost,' says Banedon, undaunted. 'There is a man who can guide us there. His name is Tipasa Edarouk – "Tipasa the Wanderer". It is he whom we must seek, for he is the only man who has ever entered the Tomb of the Majhan and lived to tell the tale.'

Turn to **302**.

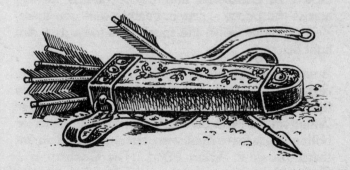

340

It takes over an hour to shake off the Adu-kaw, by which time you have been chased through most of Ikaresh. Had it not been for Banedon's timely casting of a spell of illusion, they would be after you still. You cannot help but laugh when you picture their faces, when they saw the Kalkoth leaping at them; thank the gods they did not think to question how a Kalte ice-beast came to be roaming the streets of their town.

When you have fully recovered from the chase, you leave the narrow alley in which you have been hiding, and press on in search of Tipasa the Wanderer.

Turn to **202**.

341

As you step over the lifeless bodies, you notice a Copper Key on a chain around one of their necks. Grabbing the Key, you slip it into your pocket and race down the tower steps. (Mark the Key as a Special Item on your *Action Chart*). At the entrance, you see a crowd of Drakkarim and palace guards rushing across the bridge – certain death awaits you there. You continue down the spiral stairs towards a dim light below.

A small fire, over which roasts a chicken on a spit, illuminates a guard room at the base of the tower. On the back of a wrought-iron chair hangs a Canteen of Water and a Broadsword. You may take either or both of these items if you wish, but remember to mark them on your *Action Chart*. (The Canteen is a Backpack Item.)

You hear the enemy thundering down the stairs; they will soon be upon you. However, a heavy wooden door in the north wall offers you another chance of escape.

If you wish to escape from the guard room by this
    door, turn to **246**.
If you wish to stand and fight, turn to **231**.

342

The delicious smell of freshly brewed Jala wafts from
an eating-house half-way along the avenue. Chatter-
ing voices mingle with the clink of glasses, and the
wailing cry of a hungry baby fills the air.

If you wish to enter the eating-house, turn to **296**.
If you wish to continue along the avenue, turn to
    227.

343 – *Illustration XX (overleaf)*

You are jerked backwards in the saddle as the Itikar
leaves its perch. It shrieks and caws, its wings beating
as loud as thunder. A handful of Drakkarim are scattered as if they were rag dolls as the great black bird
emerges from the pen and takes to the sky. You catch
a glimpse of a Drakkar, his death-mask slashed in two
by the bird's razor-sharp talons, as he pitches from
the landing platform and tumbles to his death in the
palace gardens far below.

The golden domes of the Grand Palace grow smaller
as the Itikar gathers speed. Soon, you have passed
over the city wall and are heading out towards the
shimmering salt-flats of Lake Inrahim. The land
below is bathed in beautiful orange twilight, as the
sun slowly sinks behind the Dahir mountains to the
west. Elated by your escape, you throw back your
head and give voice to a triumphant yell that is carried
away on the chill evening wind.

XX. You catch a glimpse of a Drakkar, his death-mask slashed
in two, pitched from the landing platform

As if in answer to your cry, an echoing chorus of shrieks pierce the sky. Fear returns to your heart as you catch sight of a flock of Kraan, hideous leathery-winged flyers. Each carries a Drakkar warrior on its back. They are over a mile behind you but they are quickly closing the gap. Less than an hour of light remains; if you can evade them a little longer, you may be able to lose them when night falls.

You must decide in which direction to fly, for you are now above the centre of Lake Inrahim – consult the map at the front of this book before making your decision.

If you wish to steer the Itikar south towards the Dahir pass, turn to **264**.

If you wish to head east towards the town of Chula, turn to **244**.

344

The old man's face is a mask of putrescent green sores. The pupils of his eyes are yellow and his ragged grey lips hang in tatters. He suffers from vaxelus, an infectious disease that rots the skin and attacks the nerves, resulting in hideous mutilation and deformity. He has been cast from his community, banished to this cave where he must eke out his last few years of life in misery and solitude.

If you possess some Oede herb, and wish to give it to the poor vaxeler, turn to **321**.

If you do not have any Oede herb, or if you do not wish to give it to this poor unfortunate wretch, flee the cave and turn to **270**.

345

You glimpse the silhouette of Darklord Haakon in the hall below, his spiked fist raised. There is a deafening crack as a bolt of blue lightning streaks from a stone in the Darklord's hand, and hurtles towards you. You dive for cover behind the body of the Drakkar as the bolt explodes. In a flash of light, the Drakkar is gone. Only cinders and the rotten odour of scorched flesh remain.

You scramble to your feet and sprint along the passage. Another bolt hurtles from the hall, tearing into the ceiling with shattering effect. Splinters of razor-sharp marble whistle down, slashing your cloak and tunic. You race down some stairs, through a silver archway and along a balcony that overlooks the lower palace. A peal of bells and the crunch of iron-shod boots echo in your ears – the Zakhan has sounded the alarm, his guards close in on every side.

At the end of the balcony is another arch and a staircase: both look deserted.

If you wish to escape through the arch, turn to **381**.
If you wish to race up the stairs, turn to **317**.

346

By the side of the street, an old man is selling an assortment of rugs and carpets from the back of a wagon. Banedon approaches him and the two converse for several minutes. Finally, the wizard hands the old man a ring; his wrinkled face beams with joy. Banedon returns to you with good news.

'The house with the blue door – at the end of the alley we passed a short while ago. Tipasa lives there.'

As you retrace your steps and enter the dingy passage, you hear the old man shriek with disappointment: the ring has just dissolved on his finger.

At the end of the alley you find the house with the blue door.

Turn to **206**.

347

Wincing from the pain of your wound, you snatch the reins back and urge the Itikar to climb higher. The Drakkar is now over a hundred feet below but he is bringing the shrieking Kraan around for another attack.

You wheel to the south to avoid being caught between the two converging squadrons of Kraan-riders. Your sudden change of direction increases the distance between you and your pursuers, but your feathered mount is badly wounded and you are close to despair; the Itikar is losing so much blood that it could become unconscious at any moment, and drop you like a stone on to the distant surface of Lake Inrahim below.

Suddenly, you spot something in the distance. It is a sight that renews your faith in miracles.

Turn to **221**.

348

Suddenly, you catch sight of Banedon. His arm is raised above the armoured parapet of the platform, and in his hand he holds a slender blue rod. A torrent of water gushes from the rod, arcing into the sky to meet the deluge of liquid flame. There is a tremendous explosion as the elements collide, and a massive whirlpool of flame and water spirals towards the Vordak.

The Vordak shrieks with terror but it is too late – its fate is sealed. The whirlpool consumes the Zlanbeast and its rider in a massive burst of sun-like brilliance.

Turn to **267**.

349

The golden blade sings in your hand, a crackle of pure energy spreading along its razor-sharp edge. You strike a tremendous blow, splitting the Vordak's skull to the teeth. It releases an awful howl of unearthly evil, pain, terror and death. As it falls, its skeletal body dissolves into a smoking green fluid, shrivelling the plants on the ground beneath.

The Drakkarim hesitate as the golden light of the sun-sword glints on their shiny black death-masks; you see your chance and run straight at them, slashing to left and right. A Drakkar raises his shield, but your blade slices clean through the iron-sheathed wood, severing his arm at the shoulder. Wheeling round, you catch another Drakkar in mid-attack, tearing open his black armour with the sword as if it were merely parchment. He screams in agony, but you disappear into the dense foliage before his body falls lifelessly to the soft earth.

Turn to **228**.

As you break cover, another burst of energy leaps from the Darklord's fist. It explodes into the base of the pillar, severing it from the floor, and the roof above caves in with a tremendous roar. The shock wave throws you to the floor, flattening you against the cold marble flagstones. You lose 3 ENDURANCE points.

Haakon's laugh can still be heard above the crash of falling stone. It rises in pitch until it fills your head with agonizing pain.

If you have the Kai Discipline of Mindshield, turn to **253**.

If you do not possess this Kai Discipline, turn to **369**.

351

As you approach the door, Banedon offers you a word of advice. 'Take care to guard your gold, Lone Wolf. Nothing tempts the Ikareshi more than a full purse. You can trust their honour, but if you trust their honesty they will steal the hair from your head.'

Inside, the mood is one of celebration. Tables have been drawn together to form a large semi-circle in front of which stands a small, broad-shouldered man dressed lavishly in an embroidered costume. A gold-mounted sword hangs by his side, its blue velvet scabbard as vivid in colour as the man's silk panta-loons. Affectionately, the man embraces his companions, kissing the friends and relatives who have travelled so many miles to celebrate his wedding. At his side sits his bride, her face concealed behind a veil of shimmering pearls. Suddenly, the tavern is filled with music as the guests take the floor for the wedding dance.

On the far side of the floor you see the owner of the tavern, a stout old lady dressed in sombre black. She watches the festivities with tears in her eyes.

If you wish to approach her and ask where Tipasa the Wanderer may be found, turn to **276**.

If you wish to leave the tavern and continue along the street, turn to **202**.

352

Beyond the portal lies a vaulted corridor leading to a grand stairway. You narrowly avoid confrontation with a dozen Drakkarim, saved by your lightning reactions. As the enemy rush from an archway on the second floor landing, you dive behind a statue of the recently deceased Zakhan Moudalla. They are so intent on their chase that they fail to notice your hiding place, and hurry down the stairs, grunting in their heavy armour as they run. Silently, you give thanks that Zakhan Moudalla was a very stout man and that his statue casts a very large shadow in which to hide.

At the top of the stairway you discover a hatch, which gives access to the roof. You climb through it and follow a path of sun-bleached tiles that wind in and out of the domes and turrets, eventually leading to a bell-tower.

You are exhausted and need to rest, your mind still full of the shock of your encounter with Darklord Haakon. The sound of his terrible voice repeating the words 'Book of the Magnakai' echoes again and again in your mind.

With desperation sapping your will, you peer out through a grille in the bell-tower. The sight before you renews your flagging hope, for it inspires a daring escape plan.

Turn to **313**.

353 – *Illustration XXI (overleaf)*

As you slay the last of the Cryptspawn, Haakon reels back as if weakened by the death of his creatures. You raise the Sommerswerd, willing the blade to discharge a bolt of power that will burn the evil Darklord from the face of Magnamund forever. The blade shimmers with golden fire but no searing blast issues from its tip. Suddenly, you realize what has

XXI. You raise the Sommerswerd, willing the blade to
discharge a bolt of power at Haakon

happened; you are beneath the earth, and there is no sun from which the sword can draw its power.

Haakon utters a terrible laugh that shakes the floor. A beam of blue flame is growing from the stone in his hand, forming a fiery blade that crackles and spits as it cuts through the dust-choked air. The stench of death and decay fills your nostrils as the Darklord prepares to attack.

Darklord Haakon:

COMBAT SKILL 28   ENDURANCE 45

Unless you have the Kai Discipline of Mindshield, reduce your COMBAT SKILL by 2 for the duration of this combat.

If you win the combat, turn to **400**.

354

You throw yourself to the deck but the axe blade strikes your thigh, drawing a crimson line across the skin. You lose 2 ENDURANCE points. Suddenly, a deafening bang rings out and the Drakkar is flung backwards, his breastplate torn open by dwarf shot. He gives a long, agonizing death-cry as he disappears from sight, tumbling into the darkness that surrounds the speeding ship.

From Barrakeesh, a roll of thunder rumbles across the darkening plain. It is full of brooding menace, as if the city itself were cursing your escape. Banedon appears at your side, his face lined with concern for your condition. As he offers a shaky hand to help you to stand, you notice that the makeshift bandage that binds his wound is soaked with blood. He is pale and weak, and close to collapse.

If you have the Kai Discipline of Healing, turn to **377**.

If you do not possess this skill, turn to **339**.

355

You roll away a split second before the mace smashes down, crushing the dark soil where your head once lay. Unless you have the Kai Discipline of Mindshield, deduct 2 points from your COMBAT SKILL for the duration of the combat, for the Vordak is attacking you with the power of its Mindforce. This creature is immune to Mindblast.

Vordak: COMBAT SKILL 17   ENDURANCE 26

If you win and the fight lasts 4 rounds or less, turn to **249**.

If the fight lasts longer than 4 rounds, turn to **304**.

356

'I knew Tipasa once, when my body was young and strong like yours. We fought the Lakuri pirates at Samiz and voyaged to a distant land where ice and snow lay thick upon the ground, and the sun had not the power to melt them. Yes, I knew Tipasa the Wanderer . . . once. All I know now is that he dwells in Ikaresh. Find the widow Soushilla – she will know. She knows all that passes in Ikaresh.'

Turn to **281**.

357

The gangplank springs up and down as you stride across the gap, and you are forced to slow your pace for fear of falling over the edge. The sentry wheels round, alerted by the noise of creaking planks. He forgets about his scattered gold and runs to intercept your attack, his spear levelled to thrust at your waist. You cannot avoid combat and must fight the sentry to the death. Deduct 2 from your COMBAT SKILL for the duration of this fight, for the plank on which you are standing is very unstable.

Platform Sentry: COMBAT SKILL 15   ENDURANCE 23

> If at any time during this combat you pick a 1 from the *Random Number Table*, you lose your balance and fall. Turn to **293**.
>
> If you win the combat, and decide to search the sentry's body, turn to **207**.
>
> If you win, but decide to ignore the body and hurry into the Itikar's pen, turn to **224**.

358

You sense that the old woman is lying. She is not Soushilla the widow – she is a fraud, attempting to fleece you of your gold. When you confront her, she turns tail and disappears into the alley like a bolt of lightning.

'Let her go,' says Banedon. 'Our time is worth more than the gold she took.'

If you wish to continue along the Avenue of Eagles, turn to **388**.

If you decide to retrace your steps to Eagle Square, you can either go north towards the Dougga Market, by turning to **376**.

Or west towards the Main Square, by turning to **216**.

359

The fatigue of your ordeal finally catches up with you; you are finding it impossible to keep your eyes open. Nolrim shows you to a bunk in the hull of the *Skyrider*. Gratefully you climb into bed and pull the blankets over your aching limbs. Nolrim apologizes that the bunk is too short, but his words fall on deaf ears – you are already asleep. Restore 2 ENDURANCE points for this much needed rest.

Turn to **300**.

360

Two black-clad guards suddenly appear on the stairs below. You are both surprised by the encounter and are slow to react.

Pick a number from the *Random Number Table*. If you have the Kai Discipline of Hunting, add 1 to the number you have picked. Now, pick another number from the *Random Number Table*.

If the second number is less than the first, turn to **226**.

If it is more than the first number, turn to **297**.

If it is exactly the same, turn to **334**.

361

Ducking beneath the boomsail, you clamber on to the platform in time to witness a desperate struggle. The blond-haired magician is pinned to the deck, his left arm skewered by a spear. With a staff in his right hand, he is trying to fend off the dismounted Kraanrider. The Drakkar senses your presence; he whirls round and draws a twisted black scimitar from its scabbard.

Drakkar: COMBAT SKILL 18   ENDURANCE 25

If you win and the fight lasts 3 rounds of combat or less, turn to **288**.

If the fight continues to a fourth round of combat, do not resolve it. Instead, turn immediately to **382**.

362

The smoke is cool and fragrant. Unfortunately, the same cannot be said of your hosts. Their long coats of dougga hide are perfumed with a musk that holds no appeal for Sommlending nostrils.

A young girl appears with a tray full of steaming Jala cups. '1 Crown each,' she says, as she places the tray upon the table.

If you wish to purchase a cup of the delicious beverage, turn to **237**.

If you do not wish to purchase a cup of Jala, or do not have any gold, you must bid farewell and leave the eating-house. Turn to **388**.

363

You dive into the garden below, avoiding death by a fraction of a second. The crossbow bolts ricochet off the poison-tipped spikes and shoot into the air, the whine of their twisted metal shafts fading into the sky.

The enclosed garden is full of the fragrance of exotic plants and flowers, clustered around a sculptured pool of deep blue water. It is a beautiful sight but one that you dare not stop to enjoy. The palace guards are sure to give chase and you must keep moving.

Ahead, beyond a tree-lined colonnade, a flight of steps ascend to a small portal in the wall of the upper palace. To your right, a leafy tunnel winds away into the shrubs and trees.

If you have the Kai Discipline of Tracking, turn to **220**.

If you do not possess this skill, you can either climb the stairs to the small portal by turning to **352**.

Or follow the winding path into the trees, by turning to **391**.

364

The room is moving, at first only imperceptibly, but in the space of a few minutes, the dwarves and the cabin have become a blur of colour. You grasp the table, your knuckles whitening as you fight to control the feeling of dizziness that overcomes you. Sounds seem distant like echoes in a cave. Suddenly, the spinning stops and blackness engulfs your senses. You have collapsed unconscious to the floor.

Turn to **380**.

365

You sense that the man's show of friendship is genuine. He may be able to help you find Tipasa the Wanderer if you accept his hospitality.

If you wish to enter his home, turn to **225**.

If you decide to press on towards Ikaresh, turn to **272**.

366

Nervously, you wait for the chance to leap up and open the door, but the crossbow bolts ricocheting from the wall and parapet are increasing in number. Suddenly, the sound of running footsteps sends a cold shiver down your spine; the Drakkarim are storming the stairs – it is now or never!

You spring to your feet and run to the door, grasping the iron drawbolt between trembling fingers. As you fight to open it, a pain tears through your back: you have been hit. Another bolt strikes home, sinking deep into your shoulder and throwing you flat against the door.

As darkness falls before your eyes, you are unaware of the Drakkarim leaping towards you, their black swords raised for the death blow. Their blades bite deep but you feel nothing: you are already dead.

Your life and the hopes of Sommerlund end here.

367

Silently, you are beginning to despair. The street is becoming narrower and more disgusting the further you go. A scraggy cat dashes across your path, closely pursued by an equally scraggy street urchin; the dagger that he carries in his hand suggests he is trying to catch his supper.

You are about to give up and suggest to Banedon that you should retrace your steps to the junction, when the street ends and turns abruptly left. A sign on the opposite wall points to the Dougga Market.

If you wish to follow the sign, turn to **376**.
If you wish to go back to the fork and take the other street, turn to **216**.

368

The axe bites deeply into your calf, making you cry out in pain and surprise. Lose 3 ENDURANCE points. However, before the guard can strike again, you lash out, sending the axe spinning from his hand. He howls, clutching broken fingers to his chest.

Gritting your teeth, you hobble away towards an open door. The air is alive with the sound of pounding feet, for the Grand Palace is now on full alert. Both the Drakkarim and the palace guard are bent on finding you; their lives will be forfeit if they fail.

Beyond the door, a bridge rises over an enclosed garden, joining the palace to a needle-like tower of white marble. At the entrance to the bridge, a narrow stair disappears into the garden below.

If you wish to cross the bridge and enter the tower, turn to **396**.

If you decide to descend the stair that leads to the garden below, turn to **215**.

369

The terrible pain causes spasms throughout every muscle of your body, making them twist and contort uncontrollably. You plead for the agony to cease. Lose 6 ENDURANCE points.

If you are still alive after this psychic ordeal, turn to **253**.

370

You sidestep to avoid its slashing beak but are caught by its talons and suffer a deep wound to your back. Lose 3 ENDURANCE points.

Itikar are wild and malicious creatures, and it can take many years for a rider to tame and train one. However, it is well worth the effort as, once trained, they become fiercely loyal to their master. The Itikar has sensed that you are a stranger, and is ferociously attacking you with its long, curved beak and talons.

Itikar: COMBAT SKILL 17   ENDURANCE 30

Fight the combat as usual, but double all ENDURANCE points lost by the bird. When its score falls to zero, you will have succeeded in subduing it enough to be able to climb into the saddle and take control. All ENDURANCE points that you lose are from ordinary wounds and must be deducted from your current ENDURANCE points total.

If you successfully reduce the Itikar's ENDURANCE points to zero, turn to **217**.

371

The axe howls through the dark; you sidestep, guided only by instinct, for you cannot see the lethal axe-blade, which hurtles towards you. Black steel bites into your side, the sudden pain making you gasp in shocked surprise. You clutch at your wounded ribs to feel warm blood oozing through your fingers. Lose 4 ENDURANCE points.

A deafening bang rings out and the Drakkar is flung backwards, his breastplate torn open by dwarf shot.

He screams a long, agonizing death-cry as he disappears from sight, tumbling into the darkness, which surrounds the speeding sky-ship. From Barrakeesh, a roll of thunder rumbles across the dark plain, full of brooding menace, as if the city itself were cursing your escape.

Banedon appears at your side, his face lined with concern. As he offers a shaky hand to help you to your feet, you notice that the makeshift bandage which binds his wound is soaked with blood. He is pale and weak, and close to collapse.

If you have the Kai Discipline of Healing, turn to **377**.

If you do not possess this skill, turn to **339**.

372

A crossbow bolt grazes your shoulder as you reach the walkway, making you dive for cover behind its low parapet wall. You lose 1 ENDURANCE point. Two more bolts ricochet from the stone lip barely inches from your head.

The stone door is shut, secured by an iron drawbolt on this side. To pull open the bolt, you will have to expose yourself to crossbow fire, for the bolt is clearly in view above the lip of the wall.

If you possess the Kai Discipline of Mind Over Matter, turn to **269**.

If you do not have this skill, pick a number from the *Random Numble Table*. If you have reached the Kai rank of Aspirant or higher, add 2 to the number you have picked.

If your total is now *0–3*, turn to **366**.

If it is *4* or more, turn to **277**.

373

'That's it!' exclaims Banedon, stabbing his finger at a map of the Dry Main that covers his chart table. 'One hundred and fifteen miles due west of Bir Rabalou; one hundred and fifteen miles due south of the oasis of Bal-loftan.' He picks up a quill pen and marks the spot. 'The Tomb of the Majhan.'

You study the map and ponder the miles of desolation separating you from your goal. Banedon notices your look of dismay and quickly tries to put your mind at ease.

'Fear not, Lone Wolf – we'll be there before the dawn.'

You smile at his confidence, but it is not the actual journey that worries you – your concern is what you may or may not find upon your arrival.

Turn to **320**.

As you tumble earthwards, a blur of colour flashes before your eyes as the Kraan-riders, the sky-ship and the distant horizon all melt into a kaleidoscope of shapes and images, which you fear will be the last things you will ever see.

You have prepared yourself for death and are calm and relaxed, when suddenly you feel your body entwined by a mass of sticky fibres. There is a terrific jolt, which leaves you breathless and stunned. The impossible is happening, you are no longer falling, but rising!

A net of clinging strands has caught you like a fly in a web. You rise up into the sky towards the flying ship as quickly as you fell. Three bearded dwarves clad in bright, padded battle-jerkins pull you aboard an outrigger that runs the length of the hull. However, there is no time to express your gratitude, for the small sky-ship is under attack from the Kraan-riders.

At the end of the outrigger, a dwarf is engaged in hand-to-hand combat with a snarling Drakkar. He is obviously losing. As you rush to his aid, another of the evil warriors lands in the centre of the craft, on top of the fortified platform.

If you wish to help the dwarf, turn to **280**.

If you wish to leap from the outrigger on to the platform, turn to **361**.

375 – *Illustration XXII (overleaf)*

Beads of sweat break out on the faces of the guards as they frantically race to load their crossbows. Your bold move has unnerved them, and their fear makes

XXII.   The other guard has drawn a steel mace and runs at you
with hatred blazing in his dark eyes

them clumsy. You reach the top of the steps and attack with the speed of a tiger, dashing the crossbow from a guard's shaking hands with your first blow, and splitting his jaw with the second. He screams and falls, toppling from the bridge to crash into the garden below. Meanwhile, the other guard has thrown away his crossbow and drawn a steel mace. He runs at you with hatred blazing in his dark eyes; you have just killed his brother and he is thirsty for revenge. Due to his frenzied state of mind, this guard is now immune to Mindblast.

Tower Guard: COMBAT SKILL 17   ENDURANCE 22

If you win the combat, you enter the tower. Turn to **396**.

376

Forty paces along this street is a barracks, a long, white-washed building with ugly square windows. A soldier sits dozing in the evening sun with his spear resting across his lap. Some children are tossing hollowed-out larnuma fruits at him, trying to catch them upon the tip of his spear. Opposite the barracks is a tavern with a line of saddled douggas tied to a rail near the main door. The braying of these sand-horses rivals the sound of revelry drifting from the tavern door.

If you wish to enter the tavern, turn to **351**.
If you wish to continue along the street towards the Dougga Market, turn to **202**.

377

Clasping your hands around Banedon's injured arm,

you concentrate your Kai skill on healing the torn muscle and splintered bone. The warmth of your healing power numbs the pain and repairs the internal damage sufficiently to be able to remove the blood-soaked strips of cloth. The wound is still open, but you have saved the limb.

'We'll help him now, Lone Wolf,' shouts a strange voice. You are surprised by this bold claim and turn round to discover who has made it.

Turn to **339**.

378

Pressing yourself against the damp soil, you hold your breath and pray you will not be seen as the Vordak glides into view. Its bony arm is outstretched, and a skeletal finger sweeps the lush undergrowth on either side of the path. You sense the Vordak is using its Mindforce to try to locate your hiding place– as the finger points in your direction, a wave of pain washes over your body. You are near to crying out, when the pain ceases; you have not been detected. The finger sweeps away and the enemy continues its search along the path.

Turn to **228**.

379

The terrible pain racks your body, making your muscles twist and contort in spasms of pain. You scream for the agony to cease. Lose 6 ENDURANCE points.

If you are still alive after this psychic ordeal, turn to **223**.

Shortly after dawn the following day, you wake with a splitting headache. With bleary eyes you peer around you at the snoring dwarves who occupy the tiny bunks of the cramped cabin. The low hum of the ship only increases the pain that throbs like a demon inside your head, causing you to wince and grit your teeth at the slightest movement of your stiff and aching limbs. You lose 2 ENDURANCE points due to this monstrous hangover!

Painfully, you gather up your equipment and climb on deck to find everything in deep shadow, for the *Skyrider* is hovering beneath a massive outcrop of sandstone that juts from the side of a mountain. Banedon still stands at the helm but he is no longer in a trance.

'Kraan-riders,' he says, pointing to a sun-bleached valley beyond the shadows. 'They arrived with the dawn.'

You stare out across an alien landscape, a mountain valley filled with thousands of pillars formed from massive and precariously balanced boulders. The pillars reach so high into the sky that an avalanche looks inevitable. The Vassagonians call this place the Koos – 'the needles'. Perched upon two of these huge rocky columns are Kraan, their Drakkar riders scouring the valley with telescopes. An hour passes before they take to the sky and disappear.

'Trim the boomsails, bo'sun Nolrim,' orders, Banedon, his voice barely audible above the increasing hum of the *Skyrider*. 'We've a fast run ahead.'

XXIII.   Perched upon the huge rocky columns are Kraan, their
         Drakkar riders scouring the valley with telescopes

If you possess a Black Crystal Cube, turn to **229**.
If you do not have this Special Item, turn to **247**.

381

You run through the arch and straight into a black-robed palace guard. You bruise your ribs and the impact throws you off balance, but you manage to grab the wall to stop yourself from falling over. The guard lies sprawled upon the floor, but with incredible swiftness he draws a shining steel axe and lashes out at your legs.

Pick a number from the *Random Number Table*. If you have the Kai Discipline of Hunting, add 2 to the number you have picked.

If your total is now *0–4*, turn to **368**.
If it is *5–11*, turn to **252**.

382

Suddenly the Drakkar screams, his limbs outstretched, his gloved hands clawing the air. He is in the grip of some invisible power which is crushing him to death inside his armour.

You step back as the ghastly sound of cracking bones rises above the screech of the swooping Kraan-riders. The Drakkar crumples to the deck and topples over the edge of the platform.

Turn to **294**.

383

You trudge through the loose red sand, your faces covered to protect them from the dust and the blazing heat. The landscape is stark and desolate; all that seems to thrive here is the wire-hard grass that scratches your boots and leggings. You soon come across a dried river bed that leads to a cave in the orange sandstone hillside. A wooden plaque is nailed by the mouth of the cave, but you are unable to understand the strange words painted on its sun-blistered surface.

If you wish to investigate the cave, turn to **235**.
If you wish to press on towards Ikaresh, turn to **272**.

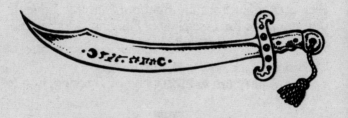

384

Unfortunately, you have misjudged how hard you need to blow to make the dart reach its intended target. The sleep dart falls short, accidentally hitting a seagull that has alighted on the edge of the landing platform. The unfortunate bird takes a few shaky steps before keeling over on to its back, its splayed legs pointing stiffly at the sky.

The guard walks over to the bird and with the toe of his boot, casually flicks it over the edge of the platform. He watches as it spirals down towards the palace gardens far below, unaware that he has only just escaped a similar fate.

Turn to **282**.

385

The seering flash of blue flame scorches your arm and face. You are thrown across the platform by the blast, and your body is peppered with shards of black crystal. Lose 12 ENDURANCE points.

If you are still alive after this calamity, turn to **316**.

386

A few paces beyond the market place, a small alley heads off to the left. At the end you see a house with a bright blue door.

If you wish to enter the alley and knock at the door, turn to **206**.

If you wish to continue along the street, turn to **346**.

If you have the Kai Discipline of Tracking, turn to **292**.

387

Your heart sinks; there are no other stairs down from the platform – you are trapped. Before you can think of a plan, the Drakkarim burst from the arch and attack.

Drakkarim: COMBAT SKILL 17   ENDURANCE 35

The only way you can evade combat is by leaping from the tower to the gardens below, a drop of over one hundred feet.

If you wish to jump, turn to **205**.
If you win the combat, turn to **341**.

388

You follow the avenue as it twists and turns through

the Armourer's Quarter of Ikaresh. A street vendor is selling a selection of swords and daggers that catch your eye; they are beautifully crafted, well-balanced and very sharp. A wooden sign displays his prices:

> Swords – 5 Gold Crowns each
> Daggers – 3 Gold Crowns each
> Broadswords – 9 Gold Crowns each

You may purchase any of the above weapons if you wish. Continuing along the avenue, you pass a meat market where carcasses of oxen are hung out in the open. You are not surprised to see the Ikareshi of this quarter walking about the streets with pieces of cotton stuffed into their nostrils (suspended by a thread around their necks), for the smell is dreadful.

Eventually you arrive at a fork, but there are no signs to indicate where the new streets lead.

If you wish to take the left street, turn to **216**.
If you wish to take the right street, turn to **367**.

389

As you leap from the gangplank on to the landing platform, the sentry wheels round to confront you. He forgets about his gold and snatches up his spear in preparation for attack. He now stands between you and the Itikar's pen, combat is unavoidable.

Sentry: COMBAT SKILL 15   ENDURANCE 23

If you win the combat, and wish to search the sentry's body, turn to **207**.

If you wish to ignore the body and hurry into the Itikar pen, turn to **224**.

390

You leap at the staggering form of Darklord Haakon, your weapon poised to strike a killing blow. However, as your arm sweeps down, a spiked fist lashes out; blood spurts from your wrist, your fingers go numb and your weapon falls from your hand. Haakon strikes again, catching you in the chest with a blow that pitches you backwards across the chamber.

You struggle to stand but the battle is over: Haakon has retrieved the glowing stone. The last thing you see before you are consumed by searing blue flame, is the evil and triumphant grimace of the Darklord.

Your life and the hopes of Sommerlund end here.

391

As you follow the track deeper into the arboretum, high-pitched shrieks echo above the ceiling of creepers and low branches. The air is as humid as a jungle. You press on but the going is difficult; the soft, sticky, rotting humus clings to your boots like river clay.

A sudden movement on the path ahead makes you dive for cover; a handful of Drakkarim are coming this way, led by a figure dressed in red.

> If you have reached the Kai rank of Warmarn or higher, turn to **242**.
> If you have not yet reached this level of Kai training, turn to **222**.

392

The ale is thick and creamy, with a taste like malted apples. You lower the half-empty tankard and wipe away the froth from your lips with your sleeve.

Pick a number from the *Random Number Table*. If your current ENDURANCE point total is less than 15, deduct 2 from this number. If your ENDURANCE point total is above 25, add 2 to this number. If you have reached the Kai rank of Savant add 3 to this number.

If your total score is now below 7, turn to **364**.

If your total score is now above 7, turn to **218**.

393

You run headlong through the foliage, the piercing scream of the Vordak tearing at your mind. Unless you possess the Kai Discipline of Mindshield, lose 2 ENDURANCE points. Suddenly, a Drakkar looms out of the trees ahead, his black broadsword, held high above his masked face, ready to strike a deadly blow.

Drakkar: COMBAT SKILL 16   ENDURANCE 25

Deduct 2 from your COMBAT SKILL for the first round of combat due to the surprise of the Drakkar's attack. You can evade combat after three rounds.

If you wish to evade combat, turn to **228**.
If you win the combat, turn to **255**.

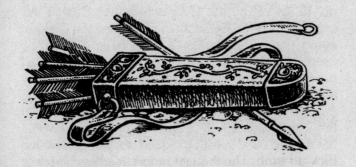

394

The Drakkar shrieks a cry of horror and lets the broadsword slip from his fingers. He claws at his death-mask, fumbling for the latch which opens the

395

black steel visor. As it clicks open, a mass of writhing insects tumble from the helmet. The Drakkar screams like a madman, as the creatures slither and crawl around inside his armour, stinging and biting his skin. In his crazed panic, he topples over the parapet and falls to his doom thousands of feet below.

Turn to **306**.

395

As far as the eye can see, a long, straight, sandstone corridor slopes away into the distance. Torches crackle and splutter on the walls, illuminating the pictograms engraved in the yellow stone.

At regular intervals, rough-edged slabs protrude into the main corridor. You stop to take a close look at one of these slabs and the floor beneath it, and come to a frightening conclusion. They are obviously traps, no doubt set off by the Giaks when they cleared this corridor of sand. Rather than instructing the Giaks to avoid them, the Darklords must have deliberately used their slaves to set them off. Once the traps had been sprung, the squashed bodies were cleared away and the slabs chiselled through to the next section. Pit traps in the floors seem to have been neutralized in the same way. Set off by luckless Giaks, they would have been filled in with the dead bodies and levelled off with sand. The thought of this heartless barbarity fills you with revulsion.

Just over a mile along the corridor, you eventually arrive at a large stone door. The stone surround bears evidence of chisel-work, but the door itself is rock solid.

You notice a faint beam of light descending from a hole in the ceiling. It creates a small circular pool of light, a little to one side of a similar hole in the floor. In the wall near to the door there is a triangular indentation, no larger than a Gold Crown.

If you possess a Prism, turn to **233**.
If you possess a Blue Stone Triangle, turn to **245**.
If you have neither of these items, turn to **298**.

396

Inside the cool marble tower, two flights of spiral stairs meet at a landing. You detect the sound of distant running feet, gradually growing louder. It is coming from one of the spiral staircases, but which one? Suddenly, a band of Drakkarim warriors appear; they are crossing the bridge that leads to the tower. You must escape.

If you wish to ascend the spiral stairs, turn to **322**.
If you wish to descend the spiral stairs, turn to **360**.
If you have the Kai Discipline of Sixth Sense, turn to **266**.

397

Greedily, she snatches the coin from her begging bowl and tests it between her blackened teeth. Once satisfied that the coin is real, she nods her head and waits for your questions.

If you wish to ask her if she is Soushilla, turn to **307**.

If you wish to ask her if she knows where Tipasa the Wanderer can be found, turn to **314**.

398
The guard raises a hand to the back of his neck and removes the tiny dart, but before he realizes what has happened, he keels over unconscious, spread-eagled on the landing platform

You can hear the clatter of running feet echoing across the palace roof: the Drakkarim have arrived. You must act quickly if you are to avoid them.

If you wish to search the body of the sleeping guard, turn to **207**.

If you wish to ignore the guard and rush into the Itikar pen, turn to **224**.

399
Banedon lowers his staff, the trace of a wry smile on his pain-racked face. 'Alas I was too slow to protect

myself, Lone Wolf,' he says, glancing at his arm. You kneel at his side and free the spear that pins him to the floor. The wound is serious; hastily you staunch the bleeding with strips of cloth torn from his dark blue robes. You recognize the robes, for they are the attire of a Journeymaster. It seems that young Banedon has achieved distinction among his brother magicians since last you met.

'It appears that we are fated to meet in their company,' he says, still watching the Kraan-riders anxiously. 'Help me to my feet, we must escape before they drag us from the sky.'

You support the magician as he grasps the ship's helm – a radiant crystal sphere with hundreds of glowing facets set on a slim silver rod. No sooner has his hand closed around the crystal than there is a tremendous explosion.

Turn to **323**.

400 – *Illustration XXIV*

You examine the floor where Darklord Haakon fell, but there are no signs of his body. The atmosphere is strangely calm and peaceful as if a great and evil shadow has been lifted.

You turn and walk to the throne where Haakon sat, waiting for you to appear. Beyond it lies a portal, an ancient inscription carved deep into the blood-red stone. Below the carving is set the impression of a human hand. Instinct and intuition guide your hand to the door; the carving fits around it like a glove.

Silently the portal slides back to reveal your destiny – the *Book of the Magnakai*. Set on a pedestal, the book lies open, its secrets revealed to your eyes alone. As you lift the sacred book, the very air throbs with the vibration of the force locked within its sun-gold cover. With a pounding heart you close the book and hurry from the chamber.

By the time you reach the foothills of the Koneshi, Banedon has successfully completed his mission; he and Tipasa are waiting for you. As they see you appear, clutching the *Book of the Magnakai*, they can barely contain their excitement.

'This night of triumph,' says Banedon, jubilantly, 'will herald a dawn of new hope for Sommerlund. The Kai are reborn.'

The quest is now over. You have found the *Book of the Magnakai* and freed Magnamund from the shadow of Darklord Haakon. But for you, Kai Master Lone Wolf, the story has only just begun.

Your destiny lies along the path of the Grand Masters.

XXIV.   Set on a pedestal, the book lies open, its secrets revealed
to your eyes alone.

400

To learn their secrets and attempt the first exciting quest of the Magnakai, begin your journey with Book 6 of the Lone Wolf series entitled:

The Kingdoms of Terror

238

RANDOM NUMBER TABLE

2	5	0	4	8	6	6	8	4	1
0	5	9	5	7	0	9	4	6	5
2	8	2	5	6	3	2	7	9	6
1	6	8	4	0	4	1	3	8	7
7	5	6	2	0	4	1	6	3	1
6	6	8	4	1	2	5	0	4	8
0	9	4	6	5	0	5	9	5	7
3	2	7	9	6	2	8	2	5	6
4	1	3	8	7	1	6	8	4	0
4	1	6	3	1	7	5	6	2	0